Once Upon a Haunted Cave

Novella

by

Meara Platt

Dragonblade Publishing, Inc. is an imprint of Kathryn Le Veque Novels, Inc.
P.O. Box 23
Moreno Valley, CA 92556
ceo@dragonbladepublishing.com

Produced in the United States of America

First Edition October 2024
Print Edition

ARE YOU SIGNED UP FOR DRAGONBLADE'S BLOG?

You'll get the latest news and information on exclusive giveaways, exclusive excerpts, coming releases, sales, free books, cover reveals and more.

Check out our complete list of authors, too!

No spam, no junk. That's a promise!

Sign Up Here

www.dragonbladepublishing.com

☙

Dearest Reader;

Thank you for your support of a small press. At Dragonblade Publishing, we strive to bring you the highest quality Historical Romance from some of the best authors in the business. Without your support, there is no 'us', so we sincerely hope you adore these stories and find some new favorite authors along the way.

Happy Reading!

CEO, Dragonblade Publishing

Additional Dragonblade books by Author Meara Platt

The Silver Dukes Series
Cherish and the Duke
Moonlight and the Duke
Two Nights with the Duke

The Moonstone Landing Series
Moonstone Landing (Novella)
Moonstone Angel (Novella)
The Moonstone Duke
The Moonstone Marquess
The Moonstone Major
The Moonstone Governess
The Moonstone Hero
The Moonstone Pirate

The Book of Love Series
The Look of Love
The Touch of Love
The Taste of Love
The Song of Love
The Scent of Love
The Kiss of Love
The Chance of Love
The Gift of Love
The Heart of Love
The Hope of Love (Novella)
The Promise of Love
The Wonder of Love
The Journey of Love

Chapter One

Cornwall, England
August 1817

"THEY ARE KNOWN as the Singing Caves, Miss Alwyn." Ruarke MacArran, the daunting Duke of Arran, surprised Heather Alwyn by coming up beside her as she stood alone on the windy cliff heights overlooking the rocky Cornwall seashore and its honeycomb of caves near his impressive home, MacArran Grange. "You must never go in them."

Heather shook her head and turned to him, only now realizing she had company. The hour was growing late, the afternoon shadows beginning to lengthen over the jagged rockface. The sun would still be up for hours. But the waves were heightening in intensity. Even now, she could hear their strident *whoosh* to shore and the soft roar as they crashed within the distant caves.

"Forgive me, Your Grace." The sound of those waves battering the hollowed-out rocks, and the siren song emanating from those hollows, had left her a little spellbound. "I did not hear you approach. I was watching the girl."

She thought she heard him sharply inhale. "What girl?"

"Oh, she is gone now. She came out of those very caves and ran down the beach." Heather put a hand over her eyes to shade them from the sun, but the young woman, hardly more than a girl, was no longer in sight.

"Dear heaven," she heard him mutter.

"Your Grace?" She was almost afraid to meet his gaze, for there was something about his dark eyes that had the power to devour her soul. It was ridiculous to feel this way about someone—a duke, no less—she had met only two weeks ago. That he even knew her name was a surprise, for he had never spoken to her until just now. But he had been watching her since this morning, and she was a little undone knowing she had his attention.

What did this fierce man want with her?

He was undeniably handsome, tall, and splendidly broad in the shoulders. His hair was as dark as his eyes, and he wore dark clothes to match. There was a brutish magnificence about his face that reminded her of the jagged cliffs upon which she stood.

Still, she did not like his ability to make *her* heart flutter.

Nor did she understand why he had suddenly taken notice of her.

Well, perhaps he made it a point to know everyone who came and went from MacArran Grange. Not that he would have reason to pay her more than a passing glance when the house was filled with guests, several of whom were accomplished young ladies making their Society debuts. She was merely serving as companion to his aunt, Lady Audley. Hence, she was no one of importance.

"I can hear the caves singing," she said, leaning closer to the edge as she watched the tide roll in. "Is this what gives them their song? The wave swells moving in and out, creating that distinct hum?"

"Yes, Miss Alwyn."

She made the mistake of looking up at him again, and immediately felt the shock of his gaze sweeping over her. There was something quite seductive in the shape of his eyes, a slight droop at the corners, as though he had just gotten out of bed or was about to lure her into it. She quickly turned away, irritated this man had the power to affect her so deeply. Why was she feeling any attraction to him?

She could not look at him without tingling, but all women responded this way whenever he was in their presence.

There was no prettiness about him, just raw maleness.

"Why did you say I must never go in them, Your Grace?" If that girl, who did not look more than sixteen or seventeen, could scamper in and out of those hollows, then what was the point of forbidding her? She met his gaze directly, a gesture he must have found amusing, if his wry smile was any indication.

His aunt had brought her here, for Heather was the old woman's companion, and her duty was to tend to her during the duke's house party. This party was to last the month, and many of his friends and their eligible daughters had been invited as well.

The whispers were that the duke was on the hunt for a wife.

Well, good luck to him.

Not that he would need it.

Even she swooned at the sight of him, and she did not really like him. Well, she liked him a little too much, but was afraid of him. His expression was always stern and forbidding, and he held himself apart from everyone. Perhaps dukes had to do this, build a protective wall to repel all those who would seek to use them.

The young ladies at this duke's house party did not seem to mind his dour nature, for they fluttered around him like sparkling butterflies hoping to gain his favor.

"Why should I not explore the caves, Your Grace?" Heather prompted him when he did not immediately respond.

"It is too dangerous." Awareness ran through her when he unexpectedly circled an arm around her waist to draw her back from the edge. "Especially for you."

She burned where their bodies touched, her turmoil prolonged while he held her for several moments longer than was warranted.

Until now, Heather thought she had been invisible to him. "Dangerous for me? Why?"

"Because you are drawn to them and the song they sing."

"That is true," she said with a nod, "but isn't everyone?"

"No. Most people have a healthy fear and avoid them. Nor would most people hear their song even if they were standing where you are to watch the tide come in." He drew her further back from the edge when she attempted to take another step forward. "This is not the first time I've noticed you here. Can you not see, Miss Alwyn? The Singing Caves have too strong a pull on you. Keep away from them. I have no desire to find your lifeless body on those rocks when the tide rolls out."

"Are you saying this to frighten me? Is this how you amuse yourself in your idle hours? By scaring young ladies?"

"I never jest about those caves." His voice was deep and resonant, reminiscent of the rumble of thunder on an approaching storm.

"Am I forbidden to walk along the beach, too?" She brushed back several strands of her hair that had escaped their braid and now whipped in her face because of the gusting wind. She did not mind, for the breeze was warm as it struck her cheeks. There was a dampness to it, too. The air was never dry around here because they were so close to the water. "Or is there harm in my taking a simple walk? I would like to understand your rules so I do not give further offense."

His nicely formed lips twitched upward at the corners. "You have a mouth on you, don't you?"

She winced. "I don't mean to."

"Yes, you do." He now allowed a full smile as he held out his hand. "Come back to the house with me, Miss Alwyn."

She stared at the masculine hand.

"Come." He reached over and took hers, interlacing their fingers in a surprisingly intimate fashion as he turned toward his grand manor. "Lass, do you know what *Alwyn* means among the faerie folk?"

"No." She looked up at him, wondering why he was holding her hand or even talking to her.

"In Celtic it means friend of elves. *Blessed* friend of elves. This is what you looked like standing by the cliff with the wind whipping at your gown—a delicate sprite about to fly away."

Her laughter caught on the breeze and echoed around them. "I was in no danger of it. All I meant to do was walk down to the beach. What is so wrong with that? Sorry, that last remark sounded petulant even to my own ears."

"I can see you are not happy with my warning, Miss Alwyn. Do you believe I issued it merely to be petty and tyrannical?"

She did not deny it.

This was her only time off, and she did not wish to spend it indoors, even though MacArran Grange was a beautiful house. The cliffs and beaches in this part of Cornwall were also beautiful, and somehow familiar, although she could not recall ever being here before. She wanted to explore as much of the area as she could before the house party ended and she had to return to dismal London with the equally dismal Lady Audley.

He sensed her reluctance. "You have no wish to go back inside?"

"No, Your Grace. Please understand, Wednesday afternoons are the only time I have to myself. I would rather spend the hours exploring, especially on such a perfect day."

He glanced toward the sky.

Heather sighed, wishing he could appreciate the beauty of this gloaming hour and the magical hues to be seen as the sun began to set. Delicate lavenders and pinks mixed in with fiery oranges that stole one's breath away.

The sky was almost cloudless today, save for a few wispy tendrils of white floating by on the August breeze. Goshawks and gulls flew over the azure waters of MacArran Cove in search of fish swimming beneath its crystal surface.

He fixed his gaze on the distant waves, appearing to study their rise and fall as the wind swept them to shore. "My other guests will be taking tea on the terrace by now."

"Other? Do you consider me a guest? I am no more than your aunt's companion."

He shrugged his broad shoulders, his gaze still on the cove. "You are a cut above a mere companion, I would say. Anyone who can tolerate my aunt as long as you have done has earned my respect."

"Oh dear." Heather was unable to hold back a light laugh. "Is she considered that much of an ogre?"

"You know she is. I'm told you have been with her almost a year now. It is about six months longer than anyone else has lasted. I marvel at your fortitude."

She blushed at the compliment, but did not pass comment.

It was not fortitude so much as desperation. His aunt was an unpleasant woman, but Heather's position as her companion was a precious salvation, and she dared not say or do anything to put it at risk.

"What do you think of my house, Miss Alwyn?" He now gestured toward the magnificent structure built of gray stone that Heather expected would stand for another thousand years.

"It is splendid," she said, following his gaze. "The roses and ivy along the walls soften it. The shutters are the deep blue of the sea and connect this house to its surroundings. I understand it has recently been restored to its former grandeur. Did you have a hand in that renovation, other than merely supplying the massive funds required?"

"Yes." He smiled again, a smile capable of melting her heart if she ever trusted him enough to be caught off her guard.

"It feels like it has your touch, a mix of power and perfection." She could not help smiling back at him. "Will you tell me more? The interior is decorated with impeccable taste. I have been in some beautiful homes, but none to match yours. The exterior is elegant, too. Every bit of its construction shows exquisite thought and attention to detail."

His expression quickly changed, and he now frowned at her. "I do not need your flattery."

"I was merely stating it as fact, Your Grace. You asked my opinion and I gave it. I would have been much less effusive if I did not like it." This man was as changeable as the wind, yet she seemed to be warming to him. She did not understand why. He still looked quite forbidding and was obviously irritated with her.

He grunted. "Follow me. We'll stay out here."

"We? Where are you taking me?"

His dark eyes swallowed her up again. "Do you not trust me, Miss Alwyn?"

She met his gaze, unwilling to lie or flatter him, for she was never one to speak falsely. "No, Your Grace. I do not trust you in the least."

Chapter Two

"**Y**OUR CANDOR IS refreshing, Miss Alwyn," the Duke of Arran said with a hearty burst of laughter. He tucked a finger under her chin, tipping her face up so that she could not avoid his stare. "I suppose I do have a bad reputation."

Heather was not certain what he would do next, but he gave a shrug and led her to a shady grove not far from the cliff where she had been standing. He stretched his big body under one of the trees, his gaze remaining on her, as he obviously expected her to join him.

"Has anyone ever told you that you look like an elf?" he said, apparently amused by her appearance as she sank onto the grass beside him. "Especially with those big, fey eyes and pointy little ears of yours. But I think you are not as delicate as you look."

How wrong he was.

She was a hollow shell inside, quite alone in the world, and scared of what might happen to her if ever she lost her position as companion to his aunt. However, she was not about to confide in him.

Instead, she patted her gown to smooth it, and then shifted slightly so that she was not seated too close to him. Theirs was a comfortable spot, hidden from view. Few people would notice them if they passed by to walk along the cliffs or down to the beach. Nor could the two of them be seen from the terrace where everyone was having tea by now, since it was on the other side of the house.

It suddenly struck her how isolated she and the duke were.

She glanced up as a sudden breeze rustled through the silvery leaves of their shade tree. "Your Grace, should you not be getting back? You will be missed by your guests."

He emitted a light chuckle. "Are you that eager to be rid of me? Most ladies would be in a swoon over my attention."

"I know," she said. "I've seen how those lovely debutantes hang upon your every word. Miss Barclay in particular."

He shrugged. "She is merely a neighbor."

"She is fascinated by you."

"Aren't they all?" he said with notable sarcasm. "What about you, Miss Alwyn? Do I fascinate you?"

She brushed a fallen leaf off her lap. "No, Your Grace. I try to avoid you as much as possible."

He grinned at her. "Yes, I have noticed."

After a moment of silence between them, he plucked a blade of grass and began to twirl it in his roughened fingers. "They think I am going to offer for one of them."

"Are you not?" She regarded him in surprise. "Then what is the purpose of inviting these young ladies and their families here? It is cruel to give them false hope."

He arched an eyebrow. "Are you admonishing me?"

"I…do not mean to meddle in your affairs."

"But you are."

Heat rose in her cheeks as she silently chided herself for spouting off at him. But having tossed out an opinion he obviously did not like, she had to tactfully retreat from it at once. "The expenses of a debut Season are quite hefty; that is all I am suggesting. Not every family can afford to put their daughters forward for a Season, much less two. Some of these girls are under dire strain to make a good match in order to save their loved ones from financial ruin. It is not fair to keep them here when they could be elsewhere attracting the attention of a gentleman who will seriously court them."

"And save them from a life of penury such as your own?"

"That is unfair...and unkind. Do you think I do not feel the frustration of my reduced circumstances every moment of every day?"

"Consider me properly rebuked, Miss Alwyn." His groan sounded quite heartfelt for a man who was reputed to have an icy heart. "I have been thoughtless in my attitude toward you and the other young ladies. You have my sincere apology."

She sighed. "It is all right, Your Grace."

"No, it isn't. I will set about correcting my behavior. Tell me, have you ever had a Season?"

She shook her head. "No, my father died shortly before I was to make my London debut."

That eyebrow of his shot up again.

"Does this shock you?"

"Actually, no. You are obviously refined. Much more so than those peahens cluttering my house right now. Gad, they are silly creatures. And do not admonish me for saying so. We both know they are."

"Perhaps it is you who are too severe."

His features lightened as he broke into an unguarded smile. "You cannot resist rebuking me, can you? Point taken. But what happened to you, Miss Alwyn? Forgive me, I know I am prying."

She decided there was no harm in telling him, since his aunt knew of her situation and would not hesitate to reveal the ugly details if ever he bothered to ask. "My father was a baronet. Sir George Alwyn, a kind man with an amiable disposition and absolutely no head for business. Hence, my present need to work to support myself."

"Have you no other family? No siblings?"

"Not that I am aware. It was my father and me for most of my life. My mother died years ago, when I was quite young. I carry a miniature portrait of her in my locket. I do not remember her at all, and would not know what she looked like if not for this locket." Heather always wore it hidden beneath the bodice of her gown, and now drew it out by the chain to show him. She opened the silver heart to reveal the portrait inside.

He leaned closer and took the locket in his roughened hand to study it. "Interesting. You resemble her, although she appears quite young. She has the look of a girl from another century. Perhaps it is her expression, or the style of her hair."

"Perhaps." She gave a wistful sigh as she closed the heart with a light snap and then tucked it back in place.

"I am sorry you lost her so young, Miss Alwyn. And your father? Did he have nothing at all to leave you?"

"He did have a little. But it all went to his distant cousin, Thomas Alwyn, a horrid toad of a man in whom my father placed too much confidence. He is a supposedly respectable landowner with a fine estate not far from ours in Yorkshire."

"Would he not take you in?"

"Oh, he was willing." She emitted a long, ragged breath. "The problem was, he turned out to be a little *too* willing. I had to constantly be on my guard and lock my door against him. His wife was not pleased by the interest he showed in me."

"Ah, that comes as no surprise." He tossed aside the blade of grass and placed his hands behind his head, resting his torso against the shade tree. He closed his eyes as the sun filtered through the leaves and shone on his face. "Did his wife arrange for you to become my aunt's companion?"

"No, Your Grace. That would have required a little thought or kindness on her part. She detested me for trying to steal her husband. He detested me because I would not unlock my door to him. My belongings were packed and I was sent away without so much as a shilling to my name. But that blame, I think, should fall upon my father for failing to provide for me. He was just as irresponsible as his cousin who has now inherited all of his estate."

Despite his closed eyes, Heather knew the duke was listening to her quite attentively.

"What did you do?" he asked. "How did you make your way to London and my aunt?"

"Lady Alwyn did pay for my mail coach ticket, I will give her that."

"To make certain she got you as far away as possible. Did she pay for your food and shelter on your journey?"

"No, she did not care if I died of starvation or exposure to the elements along the way. I expect she hoped I would. My father had a few friends in London, so the kindly coachman offered to drop me off at the home of one of them. Do you know Lord Stockwell? He is chairman of one of the London banks. A very good man with a lovely family. They took me in and secured this position for me."

"What will you do if my aunt discharges you?"

Heather's eyes widened in sudden panic.

Foolish! Foolish!

Why had she confided in this dangerous man?

"Your Grace, have I offended her in any way? Is this why you are here, talking to me now? Or have I offended you?" Yes, of course she had riled him with her loose mouth and ridiculous need to spout unwanted opinions. "Do you… Does she intend to—"

"No, Miss Alwyn." He sat up and opened his eyes to stare at her. "Calm yourself. Your position is secure. I did not mean to frighten you. It was merely idle curiosity on my part. Forgive me if my question alarmed you. I phrased it badly."

She placed a hand over her racing heart. "No, I'm sure I overreacted. It has been a year since my father's death, and I am still not used to being on my own. In truth, it terrifies me."

Oh, why had she just blurted that?

Why would he care anything for her feelings?

Indeed, he appeared decidedly uncomfortable by her admission. His shoulder muscles flexed as he reached up to rub the back of his neck. "Miss Alwyn…"

"Yes, Your Grace?" Heather waited for him to continue and was disappointed when he said nothing more.

He rose and held out his hand to help her up. "I want you to come to me if ever you are in need of assistance."

Her eyes widened in surprise. "Come to you?"

"Yes. Are you not in need of a protector? Allow me to take on that role. I want your promise on it."

"My promise?"

His dark eyes once again pierced her soul.

What did this handsome brute of a man want with her? Certainly nothing respectable, for she knew of his reputation. He was not a rakehell in the strictest sense, not one to spend his nights drinking and gambling. In truth, he was not known to drink, and his aunt had bragged he never lost a wager, although he was not much of a betting man, either.

However, he was known to go about Town with the most beautiful ladies, some of them respectable *ton* diamonds. But usually, his nights were filled with less respectable ladies of the *demi-monde*. Was this what he had in mind for her?

Protector?

He would protect her straight to ruin. "Um…thank you for the generous offer. Your Grace, I must go."

He did not prevent her from darting away, but she felt the heat of his gaze on her as she hurried toward the house.

"Heather, you fool." She had let down her guard, and this was what it led to. She broke into a run, desperate to get away from him now that she realized his intentions.

Protector, indeed.

He meant to take her on as his mistress.

Was this not what all depraved men, such as he and her father's cousin, Sir Thomas Alwyn, did?

Why else would he insist on her coming to him?

But a more distressing thought crossed her mind, for she was not immune to his considerable charms. Her body still tingled from his touch.

Those hands.

Masculine, rough, and at the same time exquisitely gentle.

Come to me if ever you are in need.

Would she refuse his offer?

Chapter Three

RUARKE KNEW HE had badly botched his encounter with Miss Alwyn yesterday, and now he could not draw near her without her flinching or finding an excuse to skitter away.

Blast the girl.

But he was as much to blame for phrasing his intentions awkwardly and making her believe he wanted to have his wicked way with her.

Well, the thought of having her in his bed had crossed his mind. But that pleasure would remain firmly in his fantasies and nothing more.

He might look like a frightening beast to the girl, but he would not hurt her for the world. In truth, he was worried for her safety.

She had seen the ghost.

Perhaps he should have told her then and there, but how did one start such a conversation when they had never spoken to each other before? *Ah, by the way, Miss Alwyn, that girl you saw by the Singing Caves does not exist. So, keep away from her because she is a phantasm who will lure you to your death the moment you draw near those caves.*

That would have been interesting.

No, he could not tell her about the ghost.

Forbidding her to go near those caves ought to be enough.

Still, he needed to watch her and protect her.

It troubled him that she had seemed to be under the enchantment of the Singing Caves when he came upon her by the cliffs. She had taken forever to notice him, and might never have been aware of his presence had he not broken the silence.

Enchantment.

The term suited the girl, for she was beautiful. A quiet beauty, not the sort to make a grand entrance and dazzle everyone. But for him, her impact was more potent. The sight of her yesterday, her dark gold locks drawn back in a fat braid down her back, and her big eyes, as green as meadow grass, looking back at him, remained vivid in his mind.

Legend had it the caves were haunted by a young girl of about seventeen years who had dark gold hair and green eyes. Was she somehow connected to Miss Alwyn? Perhaps this was why he had been so disturbed by the sight of her standing by the cliff's edge.

He needed to learn more about his aunt's companion, but this would require their spending time together. That could not happen while everyone's attention was upon him. Still, he was determined to find a way to be alone with her. He had no intention of waiting until next Wednesday afternoon to approach her.

"Miss Alwyn, get up and fetch me another sherry," his aunt commanded, purposely sending her away as Ruarke strode toward them. "Go on! Move along, girl."

The evening's festivities were about to begin.

They were in the parlor, the men now joining the ladies after having imbibed their after-supper brandies and engaged in a hearty political debate. As the night wore on, they were to be regaled by an opera singer and afterward would organize into pairs to play cards.

"A moment, Miss Alwyn."

"I'm sorry, Your Grace," she said, looking down at her toes in order to avoid meeting his gaze. "Lady Audley requires her sherry."

She scurried past him.

"Lazy girl," his aunt muttered as he took what had been Miss Alwyn's seat beside the old crone.

16

"She isn't lazy, Aunt Lydia. I've seen how attentive she is toward you. She treats you better than you deserve."

"And how does she treat you, nephew? Quite nicely, I'm sure. Have you got her into your bed yet?"

"I am warning you, Lydia. I will not hear a disparaging remark against her. If you chase Miss Alwyn away as you did your other companions, I will cut you off without a pence and discharge your entire staff. I'll wager you won't last a day fending for yourself."

"How dare you threaten me? We are in company and anyone might overhear your boorish remarks. Do you wish the world to know what a brute you are?"

"Everyone thinks it already." But he said no more, for he hadn't approached her to provoke a confrontation. "Tell me what you know about the girl's father, the former baronet, Sir George Alwyn, and his wife, Lady Alwyn."

His aunt pointed her nose in the air and gave a disdainful sniff. "I know nothing about them. Why do you care? The man was not a peer. Who knows how he obtained his title? I would not be surprised if it was through his connections in trade. I am sure his wife's family was no better. What has the conniving girl told you about them? She is one to put on airs."

He slapped his hands on his thighs and rose with a sigh. "Never mind."

Why had he bothered with the embittered old crone? She would not understand about the haunted caves or care that Miss Alwyn might be in danger. He was not even certain there was a danger. But he could not dismiss those icy tingles running up his spine when he had spotted her yesterday staring down at those caves.

"That's right," his aunt muttered. "Do not waste your time with that one. She should not matter to you. With her parents dead and no family support behind her, she is nothing."

"You are ever a delight." He left her side to mingle with his other guests.

"Your Grace!" One of the peahens sidled up to him, smiling coyly and batting her lashes as though to entice him. "Will you partner me at cards after the recital?"

He shook his head. "Alas, I must decline, Lady Sylvia. Urgent business requires my attention, and I am not certain I will be done in time to join my guests for the card games. However, my cousin, Lord Hereford, will be delighted to take my place."

He called over his amiable cousin and arranged the connection before he strode off to the next peahen and secured an escort for her.

He sensed Miss Alwyn, who had by now returned to his aunt's side, watching him. He noticed the widening of her eyes and her astonished smile the moment she realized what he was doing. Never in his life had he expected to play the matchmaker. But her earlier words had stung. He was thoughtlessly amusing himself at the expense of these young ladies.

In his own defense, he had not done it on purpose. He was serious about finding a bride. It was time he married. But none of these ladies would do. Yet instead of making his feelings clear, he had given in to conceit and allowed them to continue fawning over him.

It was not well done of him to give them hope where there was none, especially since his own bitter experiences with hurt and hardship ought to have made him more compassionate. To allow others to suffer because of his careless arrogance was unpardonable.

As soon as everyone made their way to the music room for the opera singer's recital, he withdrew to his study and searched for old books or family ledgers concerning MacArran Grange and its ghost. He found several that looked promising and opened one to read.

But it was not long before there came a light knock at his door.

He rose and strode across the room, prepared to bar entry to any peahen seeking a moment alone with him. If they thought to trick him into a compromising position, they would be the ones to suffer.

His brutish reputation was deserved, for he could be ruthless when necessary.

But there was something in the knock that had his heart beating faster, for he sensed who stood on the other side of the door before he opened it.

His little elf.

"Come in, Miss Alwyn."

He had no qualms about allowing her in.

First of all, she could not trap him into marriage because she had no family to insist on his doing the honorable thing. Nor would he ever surrender to coercion. But this girl did not need to coerce him. If her reputation were ever sullied—a possibility, because his aunt was just the cruel sort of creature to spread such lies—he would not hesitate to marry the girl.

The realization caught him by surprise.

But it should not have been all that surprising to him, for he had sensed she was someone special the moment he set eyes on her the day of her arrival.

He stepped aside to allow her in.

"No, Your Grace." She shook her head. "I dare not enter."

"Very well." He rested a hand on the doorjamb as he took in her appealing smile. "Why are you here?"

"To thank you for what you are doing."

He arched an eyebrow. "What is it you think I am doing?"

Her smile now reached into her eyes and made them sparkle. "I expected you to ignore my words, but you haven't. May I say, your matchmaking skills are excellent. I could not have done a better job of pairing these ladies to their suitable bachelors."

He responded with a light, rumbling chuckle. "I am glad my schemes have met with your approval."

"I'm sure my opinion does not matter at all, but I heartily approve. I expect your cousin, Lord Hereford, will also be grateful. He has been trying to catch Lady Sylvia's eye the entire week without success."

"He's a good fellow."

She nodded. "He seems very nice."

"Unlike me?" They were both nephews to Lady Audley, a woman who was impossible to tolerate. His cousin came from the poor side of the MacArran family and was a gentle, good-hearted soul. However, he also had the MacArran pride, and for this reason had yet to accept Ruarke's offers of a loan or other infusion of capital to help him out.

Yes, pride was a trait that ran strong in all MacArran men.

However, his cousin was obviously willing to marry an heiress such as Lady Sylvia to save his holdings. Well, he would be a good husband to that silly lady, and would not come completely empty handed to the marriage, since he had a title and several good parcels of land to offer in exchange for her dowry that would be put toward improving them.

"No one would ever mistake you for nice, Your Grace." Miss Alwyn cast him an impish smile, her gaze sweet and soft as she looked up at him. "I think it is because you do not dare show anyone this honorable part of you. But I have seen it and wish to thank you again. I had better return to your aunt."

"Wait." He caught her by the wrist, careful to keep his grasp gentle. "Before you go, I need to see you again."

She paled.

What was wrong with him? His usual prowess with women seemed to be failing him with this girl. "Do not work yourself into a state. I am not going to kiss you, Miss Alwyn. I have no intention of doing anything untoward. But I must learn more about you."

She glanced at his hand still holding her fast. "Why?"

"To be perfectly honest, I'm not certain yet. Specifically, I wish to know more about your mother's family. Did she ever reside here?"

"At MacArran Grange? How could she? Has it not been owned by your family for over a century, and much of that time in faded grandeur until you came along and restored it?"

"You seem to know my family history."

"Your aunt constantly speaks of it. She enjoys flaunting her family connections, and is especially pleased by how magnificently you have improved the family fortunes."

"But she is not pleased with me at the moment," he said.

She glanced at her wrist again, for he was still holding on to it. "Because you are paying me too much attention. She has noticed and does not like it."

"I am interested in you, but not for the reason you and she believe. Do not laugh at me, Miss Alwyn. There is a connection between you and MacArran Grange. It is a palpable bond, as though a string ties you to my home. I cannot shake the feeling that you belong here…or are in some way important to this house. Am I making any sense?"

She stared at him with those big green eyes of hers.

By heaven, she could lure a man to drowning in those emerald pools.

"I do feel it." She released a breath. "I wanted to tell you, but did not think you would ever believe me. These past two weeks, I thought I was going mad. How can I know this place when I have never been here before? The house. The grounds. The Singing Caves. All of it is so familiar. Even the song of those caves. I was humming it before I had ever heard it."

"Then my concerns are founded, Miss Alwyn. Do you have any idea why you are having these recollections and how they are significant?"

She shook her head. "No, not at all. It is a puzzle I would like to solve."

"Let us figure it out together. This is why I want to meet you again. Tomorrow, all right? Do not put me off until next Wednesday. This is too important. You know it is."

"All right." She nibbled her lip, once more drawing his attention to the lovely shape of her mouth. "These evening entertainments, much as your aunt enjoys them, will tire her out. She always sleeps in after an active night like this one. We ought to meet in the morning."

"How about sunrise at the grove of trees where we sat yesterday?"

"Yes, that is perfect. Everyone ought to be abed at that hour. I'll be there, Your Grace."

He released her wrist and watched as she hurried back inside the parlor.

He glanced up at the ceiling. "Lord, help me."

It was an odd request for a man who had lost faith years ago. But something strange was going on. Miss Alwyn had seen the ghost and now admitted the MacArran estate was familiar to her. How was this possible?

That ghost.

The smart thing to do was send the girl back to London and never allow her to return. Was this why she could tell him nothing of her mother's family when he'd asked yesterday? Had her father purposely kept his daughter in the dark?

Was it because of the ghost?

No, it was all too far-fetched.

Besides, he could not bring himself to send her away.

What irony?

He prided himself on being impenetrable, but Miss Alwyn had found a way into his heart with remarkable ease. He could not look at her without feeling her warmth penetrating its darkest recesses.

He did not like to think he was attracted to her beyond a casual interest, but he was. Nor did he wish to consider he might be falling in love with her.

Was he?

He certainly hungered for a taste of her mouth, those beautiful lips that fascinated him to the point of distraction. They were in the shape of a bow...or a heart...or a heart-shaped bow, the bottom one plumper than the top, but both of them perfect for kissing.

He groaned, knowing he would have wicked dreams of her tonight.

Very wicked.

He shook his head, irritated by these wayward thoughts, and then opened the book he had been reading on the history of the MacArran family. Several accounts were written of the infamous Dukes of Arran. He hoped they would reveal information on when the Singing Caves had been given the name. More important, he wanted to know precisely when the haunting of these caves had started.

He knew this ghost had been around for a while, perhaps seventy years or more. Few people ever saw her, but those who did described her as a girl with dark gold hair and green eyes.

Just like Miss Alwyn.

He rested his elbows on the desk and buried his face in his hands. "Heather, my little elf. Are you in danger? If so, how am I to keep you safe?"

Chapter Four

RUARKE GREW FRUSTRATED when he found nothing helpful in this first book on his family's history. If the ghostly creature wanted Miss Alwyn, then how was he to stop it when he knew almost nothing of its origins?

More important, how did one stop a thing that was already dead?

Assuming it meant Miss Alwyn any harm.

He picked up a second book and read on, hoping to learn more. A paragraph, a sentence. Any details about this girl who had drowned so long ago. He knew from local lore that her name was Bella Evans and she had lived around his grandfather's time, perhaps a generation earlier.

"Bella Evans," he muttered, "what led you to the Singing Caves that day?"

Well, he supposed most of the villagers were permitted to come and go along the beach without restriction. This still raised the question, why had poor Bella gone there that day and drowned?

Which led him to another question. Having died, why had she not moved on?

When Ruarke heard the opera singer hit the final notes of her last song, he decided to close his book and return to his guests to partake of the various card games. His game was whist, and he chose to partner his aunt instead of one of the peahens. Since Miss Alwyn was always by his aunt's side, he motioned for one of the footmen to bring a chair for her as well.

"Do not bother about the girl. Who is she to sit with us? Go away, Miss Alwyn," his aunt rudely snapped. "I shall have you summoned when I need you."

"Very good, Lady Audley." Miss Alwyn walked out of the card room, but Ruarke could not see where she went.

"I noticed her eyeing the silver earlier," Miss Barclay remarked in her smug, nasal whine that always grated. "Better keep vigilant that nothing goes missing, Your Grace."

This waspish young woman and her maiden aunt made up their foursome at the whist table. "Trump suit is hearts," he said, ignoring the comment and doing his best to ignore her, too.

This Marriage Mart business brought out the worst in some people. Cynical as he was, even he was surprised by how much bile some of these debutantes spewed. Was this how they sought to tempt him? By maliciously demeaning others?

His own aunt's laughter was as brittle as a witch's cackle. "Indeed, Miss Barclay. I have my housekeeper count every piece of my silver nightly. I am certain Miss Alwyn is going to steal it all and run off with a worthless bounder some day."

By heaven, he was going to have it out with his aunt. She had been difficult and curt with all her former companions, but he had never seen them dealt with in this venomous fashion.

He was to blame.

His aunt sensed he liked Miss Alwyn, and she disapproved.

Who was this old woman to look down on anyone? What had she ever done in all her life but take from him?

Nor were the MacArrans ever known for their piety. They had made their fortune serving as privateers in the more recent centuries, and as Varangian Guards to the Byzantine emperors in medieval times. His ancestors were little more than pirates and mercenary soldiers.

Elite, ruthless, and powerful. Not a martyred cleric or wise philosopher among them.

Was it any wonder he looked like a brute?

Or that his aunt behaved like a brute?

The evening dragged on, the rounds of whist seemingly endless.

Ruarke retired late to bed.

Never one to require much sleep, he was alert and eager to start his day as soon as the sun peeked over the horizon come morning.

He washed and dressed, hastily donning a workman's attire consisting of a coarse linen shirt and dark trousers. He was not about to take the time to dress like a gentleman, perfecting the points on an overly starched collar or fashioning an elegant knot in a tie.

He donned a pair of sturdy hunting boots and quietly made his way out of the house.

He hoped Miss Alwyn would follow soon after. In truth, he was worried she might not show up. She could not have gotten much sleep last night. Not only did she have to put his aunt to bed, but she also had to attend to the additional chores, all of them unreasonable, the old crone demanded be done by morning.

As it turned out, he need not have worried about her missing their sunrise rendezvous. She was there ahead of him, seated in wait upon a fallen log in the grove, and smiling as he approached. "Good morning, Your Grace."

"Good morning, Miss Alwyn." He settled beside her. "I hope Lady Audley did not keep you up too late."

"I managed."

He frowned. "This nonsense has gone on far too long. I am the one who supports my aunt's household. I do not expect her to dote on those who serve her, but I will not tolerate abuse. I spoke to her about you last night. I see she retaliated by adding to your woes. Did you get any sleep last night?"

"Yes, Your Grace. The chores were trivial and petty. I will survive them."

"No, I think I must insist on giving you a raise in wages," he said, partly in jest. In truth, he was the one who supported his aunt's household and was quite generous in the allowance he provided her monthly to maintain her staff and all her luxuries.

"Raise my..." She looked as though she was about to say something, but quickly clamped her mouth shut instead.

His stomach sank as he realized what else his aunt had done to the girl. "She hasn't paid you, has she? And you are too afraid to demand your wages."

Fire raged through him.

"I have a roof over my head and food to fill my stomach. She will never give me a recommendation if I leave her. Without that, I will never secure another position. Please do not say anything. What am I to do if she tosses me out?"

Her cheeks turned the brightest pink.

Oh, blast.

She was now reminded of their earlier conversation and his insistence on *protecting* her. "Miss Alwyn, it is time we cleared the air about this mistaken impression you have of me. When I asked for your promise to come to me, I was only offering to help you out. I would never be so crude as to take you on as my mistress. To be clear about this, you will *never* be my mistress."

She blushed to her roots, but let out the breath she had been holding. "Never?"

He smothered a smile.

Was that a hint of disappointment in her voice?

Ruarke intended to keep that in mind. "I only meant to protect you by securing another respectable position for you should the need ever arise. All you require is a sterling recommendation, and I shall be the one to provide it. Any family would snap you up when presented with a letter from the Duke of Arran."

She brushed at her eyes as they moistened with tears. "Thank you, Your Grace. You have no idea how much this relieves me."

"Do not thank me. I ought to have been more vigilant and done something about your treatment sooner. I promise you, it will be addressed this very day. But we are running out of time to discuss this matter of your ties to my home and the Singing Caves. I should have told you when we met yesterday on the cliff and you mentioned the girl on the beach…"

"I saw her there again this morning."

He frowned. "You went down to the beach?"

"No, merely looked out across it from atop the cliff. Is it not odd that she was there? Does she not have a home?"

"Well…" He raked a hand through his hair. "Miss Alwyn, there is something I must tell you about her. This girl… Gad, you are never going to believe me. This girl… She isn't real. You must have heard about the MacArran ghost who haunts these caves."

"Yes, but surely…" She jumped up and turned to him with her fists curled at her sides. "Your Grace? What game are you playing? Do you think I cannot tell what a ghost looks like? Some frail, wispy emanation within a cloud of smoke. That girl was healthy and real."

"That you see her so clearly alarms me all the more. Sit down, Miss Alwyn," he said with commanding authority. "I do not jest about those caves or the ghost. What did she look like to you? A girl of about seventeen with dark blonde hair she wears in a braid, just as you are wearing yours now? It is said her eyes are green, the color of meadow grass, just like yours. And she wears a plaid frock."

"My gowns are all in solid colors." She glanced at the severe, dark green muslin she wore.

"Because you dress like an old woman and not a young girl. Oh, do not be offended. You look lovely. You could wear rags and still look like an elfin princess. But you must admit, there is nothing stylish about your clothes."

"I dress for my work. I am not a debutante, merely an old woman's companion."

"We are getting off the point."

She arched a golden eyebrow. "Which is?"

"You resemble the ghost. Gold hair and green eyes. You can see the ghost and hear the song in the Singing Caves. You know my home perhaps better than I do. Why do you think you rattle me so? Do I look like a man who is easily overset?"

"No, Your Grace."

Since she had ignored his command to sit down, he now rose and put his hands on her shoulders. "Our MacArran Grange ghost is connected to you, Miss Alwyn. I am worried she will hurt you...or that my house will somehow swallow you up. I have noticed you walk toward a wall a time or two as though expecting to find a door there. I have seen you study the fireplace in the parlor as though it is out of place."

She shook her head. "Not out of place. I think something is hidden behind it."

"It was an old smuggler's tunnel that I've had blocked off, since it was in danger of caving in." He sighed. "What else do you see when you look at my house? Has the ghost appeared to you indoors?"

"No."

"Are you sure? I've seen you pause a time or two at the top of the stairs, or stop to stare at a painting. Why?"

Her eyes grew wide. "You noticed all this about me?"

He cast her a mirthless smile. "I have not taken my eyes off you since you appeared on my doorstep two weeks ago."

She shook her head. "You must have thought I was the ghost invading your beloved home."

"No, Miss Alwyn. I assure you, I knew you were very real."

"Oh." She blushed again as he rubbed his thumbs gently along her shoulders.

He silently admonished himself for embarrassing her, but not even he could deny the spark between them. "Why are you able to see this ghost? Why do you resemble her? Tell me all you know. Everything you *feel*. All of it is important."

"But I don't know anything. My father's estate is—was—in York-shire. As far as I know, I have only ever been in the north, and more recently London. I had never been to Cornwall before arriving for your house party...and yet what is happening, Your Grace? Why do I know this place?"

"The logical reason is that you must have come here as a little girl but were too young to remember."

"In this house? How is it possible?"

"What of your mother? It is likely she grew up around here, per-haps in the village of St. Austell. She might have told you stories of this place. What is her family name? Who were her parents?"

She shook her head. "I have no idea where my mother was born and raised. Even if she did tell me stories, I was too young to recall them. I don't know who her parents were because my father would never tell me. Our servants might have known, for most were in service before I was born. However, they would never talk to me about her or them. All I ever found out was my mother's maiden name. It is Evans. Her name was Bella Evans."

His heart slammed against the wall of his chest. "What?"

"Bella Ev—"

"No, it cannot be." This was too much of a coincidence to be dis-missed.

"Why are you looking at me so oddly?"

"Heather..." He gripped her shoulders tightly. "Miss Alwyn..."

"All I have of my mother is her portrait in the locket I showed you. My father would not even tell me about her as he lay on his deathbed. I don't know why he deprived me so cruelly. She might have had family in Cornwall, but I shall never learn of them now."

"She did. Your mother grew up here."

"Why do you say that? I'm sure we'll find hundreds of women with the name of Evans in Cornwall, and thousands throughout England. I wouldn't know where to start looking. My maternal grandfather could have been a peer, or gentry, or a common tradesman. A butcher or a blacksmith, for all I know."

"The local church will have records. That is the best place for us to start. But I think we must also speak to some of the old folk around here to learn all we can about the origins of this ghost and its connection to your mother."

"Why are you insisting there is a connection to my mother?"

"Did I not mention the name of our ghost?"

"No."

He kept his hands on her shoulders to steady her as he said, "Her name is Bella Evans."

Miss Alwyn's legs gave way, and she appeared ready to faint. But she recovered quickly, and her gaze was now blistering upon him. "I will never forgive you if this is a jest."

"No jest," he insisted. "Ask any of my staff or the village locals. We are not so far from St. Austell. I will take you there myself, if you wish. St. Augustine's Church is the parish church and also close by. I'll wager we find the birth records for both girls named Bella Evans there. Perhaps death records for both as well."

She shook her head. "Do you think my mother died here?"

"I don't know, but I'll wager my entire estate that she was born here. All I am saying is there are too many coincidences to ignore. Their names, your familiarity with my house. Your resemblance to the ghost who haunts the Singing Caves. Your ability to *see* her."

"If there is a connection, as you say, then what if the ghost is trying to talk to me? I should go to her and ask our questions."

"I hope you are not serious, because I am never going to let you near her." His hands were still on her slight shoulders, so he shook her lightly. "Do you understand me? You are not to go near that apparition."

"But—"

"No! What if she is the one who harmed your mother? What if she wants to harm you? How am I to protect you from something I cannot see or touch? Miss Alwyn…Heather…please, do not attempt to speak to her."

"And leave her to rot in those caves for eternity?"

Ruarke saw the pain in her eyes, but he would not relent. "Yes, if it means protecting you."

"Your Grace, it isn't fair. This poor girl must be suffering."

"Suffering? Or thriving on her murderous anger?"

"She is a child!"

"She *was* a girl of seventeen, hardly a child. She is dead now. We do not know what she is in her ghostly form. I will send you from MacArran Grange before I ever allow you near her."

Her throat bobbed. "You would send me away?"

"Do you think I want to?" He bent his head to hers, aching to kiss her beautiful, soft mouth.

"Please don't send me away," she said in a fragile whisper.

"Heather," he said with wrenching agony, and drew her splendid body against his big, brutish one.

This girl shattered his soul.

Why her?

He dared not free his heart to love her.

And yet it was probably too late.

What if he could not protect her from the unknown?

"Oh, Heather," he said, kissing her full on the mouth with scorching heat.

Chapter Five

*I*S THIS HOW *kisses feel when one is in love?*

Heather knew she had fallen in love with the Duke of Arran. How could she possibly deny it after that kiss? She knew he hadn't meant to do it, for he drew away with a horrified look. Well, not really horrified.

Confused?

"Miss Alwyn, I don't know what to say. I did not mean for this to happen." He raked a hand through his hair, then sighed and gave her cheek a gentle caress, his knuckles as light as a feather against her skin. "Are you all right?"

She nodded. "I have just been kissed by a handsome duke. Wouldn't any girl be all right after that?"

"You are not just any girl." His voice was rough and raspy as he spoke. "We had better return to the house before anyone notices us missing. I doubt any of my guests will be awake yet, but their maids or valets might be."

"Yes, I see," she remarked as he led her toward the kitchen entrance where she might slip in unobserved. She expected he would then stride in through the front entrance, for this was his home, after all. Still, caution was required. "One of us should go in first, and then the other can follow after a few minutes."

"You first. I think I shall ride straight over to the village church and inspect their records. Births, deaths, marriages."

"What should I do in the meantime? I want to help."

"My ogre of an aunt will keep you too busy to do more than tend to her whims. But it would be helpful to make note of anything that feels wrong with the house. A door out of place. A secret passage, perhaps?"

"Like the smuggler's tunnel you mentioned?"

"Yes, write all of it down. I prefer to leave nothing to chance."

"I'll make a list for you this very morning. There is a painting…" She shook her head, wanting to shake loose a memory that remained stubbornly out of her grasp. "Never mind. Perhaps I will look at it again while you are gone. Something about it feels important."

He nodded. "I won't be long."

She stood by the kitchen door and watched the duke lead his magnificent stallion from the stable and ride off. As soon as he was out of sight, she left the house, intending to make her way back to the beach, since it was early yet and she would have hours before his aunt awoke to write her list. He would be angry, but she wasn't really disobeying him.

She would keep away from the caves, just as she had promised him.

But the beach was another matter. If she and the ghost were related, would it not be helpful to seek her out there and question her?

The duke was being overly protective. He feared this ghost.

Heather did not.

All was quiet, not even a birdsong to be heard as she hurried past the grove of trees where they had been sitting a short while ago. She arrived at the cliff steps and paused to look up and down the beach. The Singing Caves were hardly visible in the distance. A mist hung over them, stubbornly lingering upon the rocks despite the sun burning down with all its heat and clearing off the rest of the beach and water.

Heather scampered down the stairs and hopped onto the soft sand. The tide was out, but she had not paid close attention to its rhythms and did not know when it would roll back in.

Well, it did not matter. She was not going to stay long, and the beach was safe even at high tide.

"Bella! Where are you?"

She did not wander far from the cliff steps, not only because she wished to keep a safe distance from the caves. Her reason was practical, for she could not afford to ruin her walking boots if caught by an errant wave.

"Bella!"

Silence.

The mist continued to hover over the patchwork of caves. In the next moment, several of its smoky tendrils began to swirl. "Bella? Is that you?"

A girl with golden hair and a plaid frock emerged and began skipping toward her. "Did you come to see me?"

Dear heaven.

Heather stared into green eyes reminiscent of her own. "I would like to talk to you. Will you sit beside me on the sand?"

Bella nodded and did a somersault before settling close. "No one ever plays with me anymore."

"Who were you playing with when you…" Heather did not want to be the one to tell the girl she was dead. "Who was with you when you last went into these caves?"

Bella shrugged. "My sister. But then my head hurt so badly, and I couldn't get up to find her."

It was disconcerting to hear her speak.

"What is your sister's name, Bella?"

"She played a mean trick on me and hurt me," she said, now frowning and breathing heavily as she began to seethe.

Heather said nothing for the stretch of a minute, but shivers ran through her as the girl only seemed to grow angrier. "How exactly did she hurt you, Bella?"

By hitting her over the head? Leaving her to drown? Was this the mean trick Bella spoke of? But who would do such a thing to one's own sister?

"Do you want to see my pretty locket?" Bella said, her anger suddenly disappearing as though it was nothing more than a wisp.

Heather nodded. "Yes, are you wearing it?"

Bella shook her head. "It is my treasure, and I keep it in the Singing Caves."

"Will you bring it out to show me?"

The girl shook her head again. "Give me your hand and I'll take you to it."

"I cannot." Heather drew her hand back when Bella suddenly reached for it.

Perhaps coming here had not been too clever. The girl was getting upset again, this time at her. Heather quickly sought to mollify her before she threw a tantrum. "Bella, please understand. I am not allowed in the caves or anywhere near them."

"But that is where I always met *him*."

"Him? In the cave?" Whom had she met? A sweetheart? Did he have any involvement in her death? "Was he a boy, Bella? Or older? A man? Was he the one with you when you hurt your head?"

"No! James loves me. He gave me the locket. I told you! It was my sister, Millicent."

There, she had accused her sister again.

But it still seemed implausible to Heather that one sibling could ever hurt another. No, she wanted to know more about this secret sweetheart of Bella's. "Dear...tell me more about this boy who gave you the locket. You said his name was James?"

"His father did not want us to be together." Bella smiled slyly and put a finger to her lips as though about to reveal a secret. "Shh, don't tell anyone. Come into my cave and I'll show you. James put his portrait inside my locket so I could look upon him whenever I wished."

"Oh, I would love to see it. But Bella, I've told you I cannot go into the caves. The Duke of Arran has forbidden it, and I dare not disobey him."

"The duke is a mean old ogre!" She tried to take Heather's hand again. "He doesn't want his son to see me."

"You met his son in secret? James is his son and the one who gave you the pretty locket?"

She nodded. "The old duke doesn't have to know. You won't tell him about us, will you?"

"He will never hear it from me," Heather assured her.

"Oh. Oh dear."

"What's wrong, Bella?"

The girl put a hand to her throat and then began to sift through the sand as though looking for something. "It's gone. My locket! *She* took it."

"Who? Your sister? But you told me you had it in the Singing Caves. You told me it was your treasure."

"It is my treasure! I had it when I went in there. Where did it go?" She let out a keening wail.

Heather's heart shot into her throat. She wanted to run, but dared not lose this chance with Bella. "Describe it to me. Let me help you find it."

"It is silver and in the shape of a heart. His portrait is inside. She took it! She took it away from me and laughed about it!" Bella's eyes began to darken as she stared at Heather. "Did you help her steal it from me?"

"No! I promise, Bella. I would never hurt you."

"Did you help her?"

Her eyes.

They were suddenly as dark as storm clouds, turbulent and unearthly.

"No, Bella. You must believe me." Heather leaped up, realizing she had overstayed her welcome. "The duke will be looking for me. I have to go."

Bella tried to pick up a fistful of sand and throw it in Heather's face, but howled when her hand simply passed through the grains like air. "You are as bad as my sister! You want to hurt me and trick me!"

Heather began to panic. She wanted to run back to the house, but her legs felt as heavy as pillars of granite and she could not move them. What was happening to her? "Bella, are you holding me back? You have to release me."

"I won't!"

Dear heaven.

"Please, Bella. Do not be angry with me. I am trying to help you. Do you know why you are still here? Do not cry. I will help you find your locket. Is this why you cannot move on, because you are missing your locket?"

Bella nodded, and then scampered to her feet and ran toward the caves.

Heather started to chase after her, suddenly finding herself free to move again. But she took only a few steps before she stopped.

Dear heaven, what am I doing?

She needed to run from the Singing Caves, not to them.

They were still surrounded in an eerie mist. She could barely make out Bella standing on the rocks and staring back at her.

Then Bella held out her hand.

Suddenly, Heather felt a jolt course through her body, and it knocked her to the ground. That granite heaviness overtook her again. She no longer had control of her limbs.

She screamed as Bella began to pull her toward the caves, as though she had managed to tie a rope around her waist along with the jolt and was dragging her ever closer.

That rope…that bond…that tie to his house the duke had spoken of.

It was not only to his house but to these caves, as well.

"Bella, stop! I cannot go in there!" She tried to pull back, but how? There was no actual rope to cut in order to break free of Bella's hold. A wave washed onto shore and soaked the hem of her gown.

The tide was coming in.

A drowning tide.

"Bella, please! You must let me go!"

Her cries caught on the wind and were carried out to sea.

The ghost had first appeared to her as a pretty girl of seventeen. But that pretty girl was no longer present, for in her place stood an angry phantasm whose eyes were as black as onyx.

Fool! Heather, you fool!

What had she done?

She stumbled as she was drawn onto the slippery rocks near the caves and scraped her knee. Waves crashed all around her. "Please, stop! Bella, let me go!"

Those jagged rocks also cut her hands as she grabbed at them in desperation.

Her efforts were to no avail. Cold water surrounded her, soaking her gown and boots. Not that any of it mattered now. Bella held a powerful force over her and was about to drag her into one of those caves.

"Bella, please. I will die if you keep me here."

The girl—or ghost, whatever it was—now tossed back her head and laughed. "Why should I care?"

Chapter Six

RUARKE HAD JUST ridden out of view of MacArran Grange when he was overcome by a feeling of dread. Why had he left Heather behind? Did she not have as much right to search those records? A greater right, if her mother was somehow connected to this ghost.

"Come on, Hadrian. Take me home." He turned his mount around and spurred the big gray to a gallop. Upon reaching the stable, he tossed the reins to his groom and then strode into the house to find her.

His housekeeper was just coming out of the music room where the opera singer had performed last night. "Mrs. Pool, have you seen Miss Alwyn?"

"No, Your Grace."

His cousin, Lord Hereford, happened to be walking down the hall on his way to the stable for an early morning ride and heard the question. "Miss Alwyn's an early riser. I saw her heading down to the beach. I'm surprised she isn't grabbing every last moment of sleep she can, considering how our aunt keeps her dashing back and forth all day."

Ruarke's heart caught in his throat. "How long ago? Recently?"

His cousin nodded. "Could not have been more than five or ten minutes ago."

Which meant she had gone back as soon as he rode off from Mac-

Arran Grange.

Ruarke raked a hand through his hair. "If she returns… If either of you see her, send her to my study and have her wait there for me. She is not to leave for any reason."

"But Your Grace—"

"No, Mrs. Pool. Not even if Lady Audley screams for her. Assign a maid to attend my aunt today." He began running as fast as his legs would carry him toward the beach.

He flew down the cliff steps and raced toward the Singing Caves as soon as his boots landed on the soft sand. No one else was on the beach, but he noticed small footprints leading away from the stairs and toward the caves.

Those footprints could only belong to Heather.

Had he not warned her of the dangers?

"Miss Alwyn!" The tide was coming in and would soon flood those caves. A mist hovered over them like an ominous shroud. "Miss Alwyn! Heather!"

The wind blew off the water in a fierce swirl, and waves now pounded the rocks with too much force for his voice to carry above its roar. One of those waves knocked him off balance and soaked him as he climbed onto the rocks toward the caves.

"Miss Alwyn!"

Surely she understood the power of the sea.

"Where are you? Heather! Can you hear me?"

He was about to call again when he heard a frightened cry. "Your Grace! In here!"

Blessed saints.

She was trapped in one of those caves. His worst fears realized.

But which one? "Miss Alwyn, keep talking to me!"

More waves, each one more intense and powerful than the first, surrounded him and soaked him with their spume. He had only a minute to find her before those waves filled the caves.

Anyone who could not swim out would drown.

And no one had the strength required to swim out, not even him…not against a crushing wall of water.

He followed the sound of her voice and caught sight of her gold hair and green gown as she fought her way to the entrance. Before he reached her, another wave crashed over the rocks and pushed her back into its dark depths. "Heather!"

He called again, his heart in his throat as he was met with silence. Then he heard a cough and a hoarse sob within the dank hollows. "Over here."

She was obviously exhausted and struggling to claw her way out. Could she hold on until he reached her?

Ruarke felt his legs being pushed out from under him as another wave rushed in and just as quickly rushed out with a forceful under-tow. But he held firm, and was almost beside her when another wave hit.

He surged forward and caught her about the waist. But they were now deeper in the cave, and Heather was clinging to a jutting rock for dear life. "Heather, let go of it and put your arms around my neck."

She hesitated, afraid to lose her grip and be forever swept into the cave's dark maw.

"Do it now, Heather."

The sun could not penetrate more than a few steps beyond the mouth of the cave. Even now, as closely as he held her, Ruarke could hardly make out her slender form. If she slipped away from him, he would never find her again.

"Heather, trust me."

She was sobbing and gasping for air.

He was breathing hard himself as he fought against another surging wave. "Don't be afraid."

She was a slender thing, and each wave was now drowning them as it filled the cave and then pulled out with a riptide force.

He lifted Heather higher so that the water did not completely swallow her up.

"You little fool," he whispered, inhaling a breath as the water rushed out again. "I ordered you to keep away from here."

She tried to tell him something, but he could not hear a word above the piercing hum now resounding through the cave.

This was the *singing* he had warned her about.

They would talk later, save the rebukes and explanations once they reached safe ground, assuming they made it out alive.

He yanked her away from the jutting rock. "Put your arms around my neck and hold your breath. This next wave will fill the cave, and this time the water will not rush out."

He kept his arms wrapped around her. She felt soft and supple against him, but he should not have been all that surprised. His body had reacted to her from the moment she stepped down from his aunt's carriage that first day.

"I'm so sorry, Your Grace. I'm so sorry."

"It's all right, Heather. I am not angry." Those were his last words before the next wave hit and held them underwater. By some miracle, he caught an ebb current and swam furiously with it so that it pushed them out of the cave and onto the treacherous rocks.

He tried to protect Heather with his big body, his back and shoulders taking a bruising as he slogged his way off the rocks with her safely in his arms. They were alive and able to breathe again, and this was all that mattered.

He ought to have been furious, for she had disobeyed him.

But she was shattered, now in tears and blaming herself.

He tried to calm her as he tumbled safely with her onto the sand and rolled them away from the rocks.

It was not a moment too soon.

Ruarke watched in horror as a monstrous wave rose out of the water and smashed against the rocks. It would have battered them with enough force to crush their bones, had they been caught.

But they were on the beach now, safe upon the warm sand as water harmlessly flooded around them and then swept back out.

In the next moment, a shrill cry filled the air, a sound as sharp as a knife, and capable of shattering eardrums. "Heather, cover your ears!"

What in blazes is that?

He had never heard such an anguished wail before, certainly nothing like it ever emanating from the Singing Caves.

It had to be the keening shriek of a raging ghost.

Ruarke wasted no time in carrying Heather to the cliff steps. But he had to set her down by the time they reached the stairs. His lungs were burning so badly, he thought they might burst.

His arms gave out, as did the rest of his body.

"We are done for if she comes after us." He set her down with a grunt and dropped onto the sand beside her, completely spent.

She sat on the bottom step and let the tears stream down her face.

"Stop crying, lass." His voice was little more than a rasp, as he needed several moments to catch his breath.

"How can I?" She took in sobbing gulps of air. "We almost died. It is all my fault."

They were soaked to the teeth, and Heather was shivering.

The pain of a thousand agonies was etched on her face as her gaze met his. "I am so sorry. I never meant—"

"I do not want to hear another *sorry* out of you," he said with a growl of frustration, still shaken by how close they had come to dying. "Did I not warn you to stay away? Now do you believe those Singing Caves are haunted and dangerous?"

"I always did believe. But I saw her. I saw Bella and spoke to her."

Blast the girl.

"You spoke to a ghost?" His question came out in another low growl.

Her eyes widened. Beautiful eyes of softest green. "Yes. Please, let's get away from here and I will tell you everything."

He rolled to his knees and took another moment to rise to his full height. It was a struggle, but Heather was also struggling. He looked down at her pathetic form and brushed back several strands of her hair that were now stuck to her cheeks. "You're shivering and your lips have turned blue."

She nodded and rose shakily.

He did not have a jacket to wrap around her, since he'd gone off to the church in the work clothes he had been wearing when meeting her in the grove earlier. But she was still shaking, so he put an arm around her shoulders and held her close. "I know I am sopping wet, but the heat of my body might warm you a little."

"I don't deserve your kindness."

What was he to do about her?

Kindness? He was in love with her, and his heart was aching with the knowledge he had almost lost her.

But he was also furious.

Her shoulders slumped and she lowered her head, about to cry again.

"Blast it, Heather. What is wrong now?"

"How are we to avoid tongues wagging when we walk in looking like two shipwreck victims?"

He did not know and did not care. He could walk into his home stark naked while talking gibberish and all would be overlooked because he was a duke. But Heather's reputation would be lost, he supposed. Especially with her gown clinging to her every luscious curve.

This girl had a body that could stop a man's heart...or make it speed up to the point of bursting.

She was slender and delicate, and obviously too drained from her near-death escape to make it up the stairs. They had not climbed more than five steps before she faltered.

"Heather," he grumbled, and hoisted her over his shoulder as a farmer might hoist a sack of grain. It was not in any way romantic, but his arms were numb and he would drop her if he had to carry her in his arms as though he were a gallant lover.

She ought to be grateful he had her slung over his shoulder.

"What are you doing?" She tugged lightly on his hair. "Your Grace, put me down. We'll be seen by your guests!"

"I am not putting you down," he muttered, tightening his hold on her. "Of all the stupid, thoughtless—"

"I thought you said you weren't angry."

"I lied. We were about to die, and I did not want our last words to each other to be filled with ire and resentment. But we've made it out alive. I am so furious with you right now, I want to wring your little elf neck. What were you thinking? Did I not tell you to keep away from the caves? Not five minutes later, you are running toward them."

"She came to me on the beach! I asked her questions, but we were only seated on the sand. I did not go anywhere near the caves."

"Then how did you end up in one of them? Were you magically transported?"

"Something like that." She tugged on his hair again. "Will you put me down? I am not a sack of grain to haul over your shoulder. I would rather not have you talking to my backside."

"And I would rather not have you soaking wet and almost drowned." Although he did not mind the soaking-wet part so much, since her body was exquisite. It was the fact she had almost drowned that had him seething. "Why were you at the caves?"

"Bella became angry with me, and...I did not realize ghosts had this power, but she pulled me into them."

"Pulled you in?"

"Yes, as though she had a rope attached to my soul. Then her eyes turned a horrid shade of black, as dark as obsidian or onyx."

"For pity's sake." He shifted her more securely over his shoulder as she struggled to free herself. "We are both going to fall if you do not stop wriggling, and I shall likely land atop you. I have no wish to squash you."

"Just let me go."

"So you can run back to your ghost and ask her more questions?"

"No! I've learned my lesson. I dare not go near her again. Besides, I gave you my word."

"And you expect me to trust it now? Oh, hell. Do not start crying again."

"I never meant to break my promise."

"But you did."

"I know, and I shall be eternally ashamed of it. But I learned something very important. Bella did not go into the caves alone."

"Heather, do not start—"

"No! Do not cut me off. This is too important. Her sister was with her. I think she hit Bella over the head and left her there to drown. Do we know what happened to the sister? Maybe this is why Bella haunts the Singing Caves, because no one realizes she was there with Bella and got away with murder. I think she stole her necklace, too."

"Stop talking, will you?"

"Why? Does it not all start to make sense?" She gasped as they neared the house. "What made you turn back? Weren't you on your way to the church to read the birth and death registers?"

"I had a bad feeling about you, so I rode home. Good thing I did."

"Did you see Bella? She was in the cave with us."

Lord, this girl was shooting shivers up his spine. "No, just you."

"Perhaps you scared her off."

He set Heather down and took her by the shoulders. "Do you think that apparition is afraid of me? I can assure you, it is not. Do not be fooled by the fact it appears in the form of a pretty girl. It is no longer a corporeal being. It could be anything, a creature merely using poor Bella's form to lure innocents like you into the Singing Caves. I am worried you do not seem to be nearly as afraid of it as you ought to be."

"Not afraid? Did I not just describe her shockingly onyx eyes to you?" She made a sound somewhere between a cough and a huff. "I was always afraid. But I ached to know about my mother, whether she and Bella were related. This was more important to me than my fear. There is such an emptiness in my soul, as deep and dark as an abyss. Why would my father not tell me about my mother?"

Ruarke understood the reason. Was there any doubt now? Her father was afraid this ghost would try to claim Heather, as it had tried years ago and almost succeeded in doing a few minutes ago. It was the only thing that made sense. He wanted to protect the daughter he loved.

The girl Ruarke now loved.

Blessed saints.

Was this what he was feeling? Mad, wild, fierce love?

"Your Grace, I am in imminent danger of being seen with you and having my reputation put in tatters."

"You run no risk of that." He ignored her little cry of outrage as he hauled her over his shoulder once again to carry her into the house. "I'll make certain it is put right, should your good name suffer. I've told you I will protect you."

"How? By ruining me and giving me no choice but to become your mistress?"

Chapter Seven

HEATHER'S HEART ACHED so badly, she could hardly breathe. "Your Grace, you said you would not kiss me, but you did. You said you would never make me your mistress, but... And now you think you can because I let you kiss me, and then kissed you back."

Bella's ghostly laughter began to ring in her ears again, and she could not make it stop. This was tragic, not funny. She did not want to be any man's paramour, not even this one whose skin held the scent of bay spices and whose muscled arms felt like heaven.

She moaned. "I can hear Bella. She is laughing at me."

"Bloody blazes." He strode into the house through the kitchen, putting the scullery maids in a dither as he marched in with Heather tossed over his shoulder, both of them soaking wet. The hour was still early, and there could not have been very many people stirring. "Anyone utters a word about seeing me with Miss Alwyn, and you will *all* be sacked. Understood?"

Heather tried to kick him. What a cruel thing to say to those poor ladies! Was their life of drudgery not misery enough?

He carried her into his study and practically dumped her onto one of the tufted leather chairs before striding to the door to bolt it.

Her eyes widened as, having securely closed them in, he now approached her with a menacing stride. "Your Grace, what are you doing?"

His shirt was pasted to his body, revealing every exquisitely detailed bulge of muscle and sinew. His hair was slicked back and his expression was as granite-hard as his incredible muscles.

He planted his hands on either side of her chair and leaned in close, his dark eyes blazing. "I am trying to save your life. What do you think I am doing? Must I lock you away to keep you safe?"

"No! That is outrageous. And now everyone will know I am in here with you and believe all manner of sordid activities are going on because you've bolted the door."

"Are you berating me?"

She pursed her lips. Why was he being so stubborn? "I am merely pointing out the obvious. Will you allow me to return to my quarters and change out of my wet gown? You ought to do the same, because the water was cold and you will catch a chill if you are not careful. Besides, I am sure I am ruining the leather on your beautiful chair. Not to mention your big, wet boots tromping on the carpet."

"You are still berating me."

"I am showing concern for you. Do you think my heart is not aching because of my mistake? I completely misjudged Bella's strength and almost got you killed because of it. It is one thing to be stupid and hurt myself, but unforgivable to hurt others. I am truly sorry I ever went down there... Well, not completely sorry. Actually, not sorry at all, despite her almost killing me. I believe she wants my help."

"She has an odd way of asking for it." He eased back with a groan. "You are coming with me to the parish church. I dare not let you out of my sight again. *Not ever.* And do not utter another word about your ruination. Most of my guests will still be abed and not thinking of you or wondering if you and I are down to breakfast. I have already arranged for one of my maids to attend my aunt if she happens to wake before we return."

"You don't mind having me with you at St. Augustine's? I do not understand how you can stand to look at me after what I've done.

Well, I am grateful, even if you only want me there because you do not trust me."

"I do trust you, but I haven't calmed down yet over that *thing* who tried to drown you," he said.

"Bella isn't a *thing*. We must find out all we can about her and her sister, and their connection to my mother."

"Run up and change. I'll meet you in the entry hall in a few minutes."

"Your Grace, what about my reputation?" she asked. "I know you don't wish to discuss it, but I cannot be seen leaving with you."

"I've assured you that you won't be seen. Only my cousin is awake, and he will not breathe a word."

"And what of our return? Everyone will talk when we walk in together. It is already a disaster that your scullery maids saw us. And it was very cruel of you to threaten them."

He arched an eyebrow, the gesture making him look handsome and sinister at the same time. "I have no intention of discharging them, if this is what worries you."

"You don't? But they do not know this and must be cowering in fear."

"That's right, as they ought to be. I want them to believe I am serious. How else will they keep silent? It is no one's business what I do or whose company I keep."

"Are you not listening? If I go with you to the church, then everyone will know we have been together. All tongues will wag. Your aunt will give me the boot, and rightfully so. Everyone in Society will hear of it because you are a bachelor duke and they are all fascinated by you."

"Do you think I care?"

"Obviously, you don't. But it is my good name at stake, so I care very much. Women drop at your feet or, more accurately, fall into your bed. All you have to do is nod in their direction and they come running. This is what they'll think I have done. Who will hire me then? And what good will your recommendation be? They'll all think you gave it because I was your...*you know*."

He appeared irritatingly calm about the whole thing as he said, "I have a solution for that problem."

"I do not want to hear your solution," she said, truly uncomfortable for the droplets falling on her nose and running down her neck. She hoped the seawater had not permanently ruined her gown and boots, for she could not afford to purchase replacements. "I will not be your mistress."

"I had no such thing in mind."

"Then do you think to fob me off on one of the bachelors at your party as you have done with your peahens? Your matchmaking skills won't work for me because I haven't a shilling to my name, or any worthwhile family connections."

"I know of someone who will take you exactly as you are."

"Then he is an idiot." She frowned, truly weary of this pointless discussion. Yes, she wanted to go to the church with him and explore their records. But she did not think the risk was worth it. She would go on her own next Wednesday on her afternoon off.

What a hideous morning this was turning out to be. What could he possibly say to her to make things better?

He emitted a deliciously soft laugh. "An idiot, is he?"

She nodded. "Utter and complete. Not even *I* would marry me if given the chance."

"Heather, you are priceless," he said with a glint of mirth in his eyes. "Come to church with me."

"And be ruined?"

"Do not be dense." He ran his knuckles lightly along her cheek in an achingly sweet caress. "To arrange for the banns to be read. What if I were the one to marry you?"

She stopped breathing.

Truly, she could not catch a breath. "You would marry me?"

Was *he* real? Or had the ghost taken over his body?

"You don't believe me. Must I kiss you again?"

She nodded, for one should be able to tell if a cold, dead thing had its lips on yours.

He drew her out of the chair and wrapped his arms around her. "Your Grace, I—"

"Be quiet, Heather." His beautifully shaped mouth closed over hers with unexpected heat and a possessive hunger.

Her bones turned liquid, which was appropriate, since they were both soaked to the skin. There was something scorching and shocking about their wet bodies pressed together.

Sweet mercy!

What was she thinking?

She pushed out of his arms with a sob.

"Oh, my elf princess. Do not doubt that I am offering to marry you. Will you have me, Heather? Will you have me for your husband?"

"Then you are serious?"

He nodded and held his arms out to her. "Upon my oath."

As his words sank in, every moment of strain and fear since her father's death suddenly poured out of her. She flung herself in his arms and began to shed tears in earnest. She hadn't dared cry since the day her father passed and she learned he had left her with nothing.

She still loved her father.

But did she not also have the right to be angry with him for leaving her so abandoned?

The duke kissed her brow. "No more tears, for I have you now, and no one will ever hurt you again."

She looked up at him, knowing he had to care something for her or he never would have made the offer. But he was also quite honorable and probably blamed himself for being somehow responsible for the ghost. Just because the caves were on his property? How could any of this be his fault? Or was his offer prompted by pity?

"I cannot think when I am around you," she said in a ragged whisper, no longer caring to know the exact reason. "I cannot breathe. Will you be angry if I tell you that I am in love with you? It cannot come as a surprise, since I doubt there is a woman alive who does not feel this way about you."

"As long as you are among them," he said with a chuckle. "I think it is time you called me Ruarke."

She nodded. "Ruarke...*Ruarke*. I tried so hard to avoid you. I thought you were curt, brooding, arrogant, and I did not want to like you. But my heart had other ideas. It is awful that your every frown or scowl or obnoxious tip of your chin endeared you to me all the more."

"Heather," he said with a soft laugh, "I don't know whether to love *you* all the more or feel insulted."

She emitted a ragged breath and smiled up at him. "Please, love me. Do you think it is possible someday? For I have lost my heart to you and love you so very much."

He kissed her softly on the mouth. "Yes, Heather. It is quite possible."

Chapter Eight

RUARKE WAS NOT certain how it had come to this. Marriage. Nor did he know how he would feel or how he *should* feel now that the matter was resolved.

He was a betrothed man.

He waited for the moment of dread to hit, the realization he had made a mistake. But it never came. The decision to marry Heather Alwyn turned out to be an easy one for him, as he sensed it would be the moment he had set eyes on her.

There was a softness to the girl, a vulnerability he could so easily have used for his own selfish ends. Instead, all he wanted to do was wrap her in his arms and protect her. Make a life with her. Perhaps find the happiness that had always eluded him.

But first, they had to get rid of the ghost.

He strode downstairs after changing his clothes, and went to wait by the entry hall to meet her. She was already there, staring at the portrait of a former Duke of Arran, his granduncle, James. He watched as she drew out her locket and held it up to his portrait. "What do you see, Heather?"

"Look at the lockets, mine and the one in this painting."

Ruarke drew in a breath. "This is why it drew your attention. I never noticed what he was holding in his hand. I thought it was a watch fob, but it is her locket."

"Not Bella's locket, but one to match it. Bella's had a portrait of him inside. The one he is holding is open to reveal a portrait of a girl. No doubt it is Bella. But look at my locket. It is the same girl. It is *his* locket."

She turned to Ruarke in dismay. "I have been wearing it, thinking it held a portrait of my mother. But this is James's Bella. He is the boy she loved... Well, before he inherited the dukedom. She knew him simply as a young man and heir. I have been wearing Bella close to my heart all this time. But what of my mother? And how did I come to possess his locket?"

Ruarke placed an arm around her shoulders. "Perhaps we'll find the answers at the parish church."

He walked her to the stable and helped her into the curricle standing in wait beside it. They rode in silence, each of them lost in their thoughts. It was not long before the spire of St. Augustine's Church came into view.

"We're almost there, Heather." Ruarke flicked the reins to urge the matched grays forward. Within moments, he would be arranging for the banns to be read, and next they would review the parish records.

Heather cast him a hesitant smile when they arrived, and he held out his arms to help her down.

"I am of a mind to obtain the license and simply be done with it," he said. "I mean, be done with the agony of waiting. I have no second thoughts about marrying you."

She shook her head. "I do not understand why you are so sure of me."

"Do you prefer to wait?"

"No, I would marry you today if I could. It is *your* haste that troubles me."

"Stop trying to talk me out of marrying you."

"I'm not. You are my dream come true. Almost too good to be

real. Have you considered that our ghost may have cast a spell over you? Think hard before you say anything about posting the banns, Your Grace."

"Ruarke. Call me Ruarke. And no, that *thing* has not cast any love spell over me."

"How can you be certain? Oh, I suppose it is because you are not in love with me. Perhaps a little lustful and overly protective?"

He laughed. "Is this how I appear to you?"

"Your eyes smolder when you look at me, and then there is your rakish smile." She sighed. "Let's see what the church records turn up."

The vicar, an older gentleman by the name of Felix Orman, met them at the door of the church. "Do come in, Your Grace. Ah, and you have a lovely companion with you. Welcome, my dear. To what do we owe the honor?"

"A wedding," Ruarke said, placing Heather's arm in his. "Miss Alwyn and I are officially betrothed and would like to have the banns read starting this Sunday."

"What joyous news! Come into my study and we shall make the arrangements." Orman waved them on, gesturing for them to follow him through the church. It was a typical house of worship for these parts, not too big, but well maintained, and had beautiful stained-glass windows that cast light of many colors onto the pews. "So, you have decided to marry here?"

Ruarke nodded. "Yes."

"You do us a great honor. Goodness, how did you manage to keep your courtship quiet? News spreads through our village like wildfire. The gossips certainly got it wrong this time, did they not? We thought your house party was held for the purpose of finding yourself a bride. But you must have had Miss Alwyn in mind all along." Orman motioned them past the pews and beyond the altar toward a door at the rear. "How else would the betrothal contracts be so quickly put in order? Solicitors are a solemn lot and know how to keep secrets. Well,

I suppose it was all taken care of in London."

"Quite in order. Nothing to be done but marry Miss Alwyn." Ruarke ignored Heather's light pinch to his arm. She was irritated with him for making their betrothal seem official when no contract had been drawn up for her to sign. She would howl when he took her to the bank and opened an account for her.

He intended to deposit a sinful sum, for he refused to have her at anyone's mercy ever again. She was too intelligent and had too much spirit to be chained like an ox to toil for undeserving souls such as his aunt.

"It is also possible I will simply acquire the license and marry Miss Alwyn within the week," he said, smothering a chuckle when she pinched him again. "Will it take long to prepare the license?"

"Assuming we decide not to wait," Heather added with a light frown up at him. "Which has not been decided upon at all."

The vicar looked from one to the other in mild confusion. "I'll ask my wife to serve tea and refreshments, and we shall discuss whatever arrangements you wish to make."

Ruarke turned to Heather once the vicar had rushed off to find his wife.

"Pinch me again, my little elf," he said with a grin, "and I will insist he marry us here and now."

"I knew it." She stared at him with her lovely eyes wide. "You are under a spell."

"I am not, I assure you."

"Then tell me, why are you convinced I am the right woman for you?"

"You have a nurturing heart."

"And?"

"What more need I say?"

"I don't know. Should there not be something more?"

"Not for me." He cupped her face in his hands and gave her a soft kiss on the lips. "Everyone believes I have led a charmed life, but my early years were brutal and filled with beatings. My father was not a kind man, and my mother was at best indifferent. Lady Audley is my father's sister and cut from the same abusive cloth. Is it any wonder she treats you as she does? I am only glad she has not beaten you."

"I think I would have hit her back if she tried," she said. "That would have been a step too far even for a wretched companion such as myself. But how could your parents do this to you? To hurt a child? Their own child? It is beyond cruel."

"For whatever insane reason, my father believed he was beating strength into me. I made myself a vow never to permit anyone to raise a hand to my children. I promised myself that they would be loved as I never was. I do not need my wife to be a dazzling showpiece who has no compassion or understanding of another's suffering. I want someone who is kind to the core, whose instincts are to help and nurture. Who cannot bring herself to be cruel. I saw those traits in you immediately."

She shook her head and gave a shaky laugh. "You are describing the attributes of an excellent nanny."

"I never desired a single one of my nannies." He cast her a wry smile. "They were all hideous. But you are lovely."

"It does not feel like enough reason to marry me."

"Because you think I can get away with less? Is this all you want? To be my mistress."

"No!"

"Then why are you trying to talk me out of marrying you?"

"I'm not. I am merely trying to make sense of my good fortune. Oh, I hear the vicar returning."

Ruarke understood her hesitancy.

She needed to hear that he loved her, not a vague promise to love her in the future. But his scars cut deep, and he could not yet admit his feelings. It was enough for now. Let her believe he was marrying her out of whatever reasons satisfied her.

She would soon understand how deeply he cared for her.

Theirs would be a love match, just as a match between James and Bella would have been had circumstances not prevented it. In this regard, he was much like his granduncle, a man who loved deeply and faithfully. James had never married. Ruarke now understood the reason why.

He had only ever loved Bella.

Upon James's death, the dukedom had passed down through the younger brother's line, Ruarke's grandfather first coming into the title, then his father, and finally himself.

Ruarke acceded to Heather's request and agreed to the banns being read for three Sundays in a row. He knew she was insisting on it for his sake, to give him time to back out if something awful turned up in her family history.

Having completed the marriage arrangements, Ruarke now began asking questions about the ghost.

The vicar blanched. "You've seen her, Miss Alwyn?"

"Yes, on the beach. She was coming out of the Singing Caves. What can you tell us about her?"

"Me?" He mopped his brow. "I am fairly new to the area, assigned here only fifteen years ago. But my curate was born and raised not far from here in the village of St. Austell. Let me find him."

He scurried off again.

"He looked ready to pass out when we mentioned the ghost," Heather remarked.

Ruarke took her hand. "Because he has a healthy fear of it."

They did not have long to wait before the vicar returned with his curate, an elderly man who looked somewhere around fifty or sixty and whose name was Simon Cornwake. The vicar's wife rolled in the tea cart and offered each of them a cup of tea and raisin cake. "How lovely," Heather said, and smiled at the woman.

Since the vicar's wife appeared to have no intention of leaving them to their privacy, Ruarke decided to let her remain. In fact, she could be helpful to the discussion. Women always knew more about family histories than men did. "When did the ghost first come into being, Mr. Cornwake? Do you know who the girl is exactly? It is common knowledge her name is Bella Evans. But who was her family? Were they of importance in the area? Were any questions raised regarding the manner of her death?"

The curate took a sip of his tea and then set down his cup. "I shall do my best to answer all your questions, Your Grace. Just keep in mind that most of my knowledge is gossip handed down from my grandparents to my parents, and now to me."

Heather squeezed Ruarke's hand. He covered it with his own as the curate began to relate his story.

"My grandmother was only a girl when it happened, but she knew Bella. They were neighbors and schoolmates. According to her, Bella was a lovely child. She never put on airs, even though her father was the local magistrate and quite prominent in the area."

"Bella is also my mother's name," Heather said. "Bella Evans was her maiden name. I think she might have been born here."

"And possibly died here," Ruarke added, putting an arm around her. "We hope your records will tell us all we wish to know. Miss Alwyn's mother might have been named after this very ghost."

"But our ghost also had a sister," Heather added. "Do you know what happened to her?"

"Millicent? She was a half-sister to Bella," Cornwake said. "The magistrate's first wife died several years after giving birth to Millicent. She was their only child. He married Bella's mother about a year later. Several years after that, Bella was born. They were the magistrate's only children, two girls about six years apart in age."

"What happened to the elder daughter, Mr. Cornwake?" Heather asked.

"Oh, Millicent went on to marry a Barclay. You must know the current Miss Barclay, Your Grace."

Ruarke nodded. "She is attending my house party."

"A most unpleasant young lady," the vicar's wife muttered.

The vicar cast her a warning glance. "My dear! You must not speak unkindly of our parishioners."

"I am only saying what is true."

Ruarke was curious. "Tell me, Mrs. Orman. I expect we hold the same opinion of her, but what has she done to make you think this of her?"

"She is a sneaky thing. Always jealous of others and not above accusing someone of misdeeds if she considers them a rival. I think this trait must run in her family. Her mother is the same way. Just last week she made a fuss about her gloves being stolen when—"

"Please, my dear," the vicar said. "She found them and all is well."

"Millicent was also a sneak, according to my grandmother," Cornwake interjected. "She claimed Millicent was terribly jealous of Bella. After the younger sister died, Millicent was the only child, and her father doted on her. Miss Alwyn, I see you are frowning."

"Is it possible Millicent was with Bella when she drowned? What did your grandmother tell you of that day?"

He shook his head. "She always thought it odd that Bella lost her life in those caves. Bella was an adventurous girl, but understood the tides. Everyone in these parts did, for anyone raised near the sea learns early to respect its power. That's what always troubled my grandmother. Bella would never have gone to the Singing Caves at high tide. No, Your Grace. My grandmother was adamant about that."

"Was there an investigation conducted?" Ruarke asked.

"Yes, but nothing ever came of it. An inquest was held, led by the Duke of Arran, your very own great-grandfather, but he determined her death to be accidental. The girl slipped and hit her head, that was the ruling. My grandmother never believed it. She had seen Millicent walking to the beach with Bella that afternoon."

"Did she report this to the duke?" Heather asked.

"Yes, but Millicent insisted she had returned home and not gone down to the beach or the caves with her sister. There were no witnesses to contradict her statement. It was a sad day for the village. Bella was a beautiful girl with golden curls and sunshine in her smile. She had eyes as green as an Irish meadow. Those are my grandmother's exact words." Cornwake paused a moment to stare at Heather. "Miss Alwyn, I could be describing you. Well, there is nothing more to tell."

"What of the other Bella Evans, Miss Alwyn's mother?" Ruarke asked.

The curate shook his head. "I'm afraid I don't know anything about her. She could have lived here, but I was sent off to school as a boy, and then continued my studies at Oxford. There are gaps in my knowledge of our little corner of Cornwall."

"May we look at the registers now?" Heather asked.

The vicar rose. "Yes, of course. Let me bring them in here for you."

He and the curate piled four massive books upon the vicar's desk, then left Ruarke and Heather to their reading. It did not take Ruarke long to find the birth record of Heather's mother, and to his surprise, the record of her marriage to one Sir George Alwyn, baronet. "Heather, here it is. All of it, including the names of your maternal grandparents, Joseph and Sarah Evans. See, it is right here."

She put a hand over her heart. "Is there a chance my grandparents are still alive?"

He glanced at the book of death records. "We could spend time searching through that tome, but I think Mrs. Orman is the one to ask."

He took a moment to step out of the room to call for her. "Mrs. Orman, can you tell us anything about Miss Alwyn's grandparents,

Joseph and Sarah Evans?"

"Oh, indeed. Yes, I can. I had no idea they were related to you. How dense of me not to make the connection. But I never heard either of them speak of a daughter or a granddaughter. I thought they had no children. How odd… Well, they passed on quite a few years ago. It was not too long after we arrived."

Ruarke took hold of Heather's hand, knowing how deeply she must be feeling their loss. "It should not be too difficult to learn more of your mother's ancestry now that we know who her parents were."

"Why did my father never tell me about them? And why would my grandparents never mention me or my mother to Mrs. Orman?" She furrowed her brow as she continued to look at him. "It feels as though they wanted to hide all connection to me."

"To protect you, Heather. I'm sure they loved you. But what if you came here as a child and saw the ghost? Or were somehow drawn into the Singing Caves and almost lost your life? It would have frightened them. Look, here…in this entry. Bella and Millicent Evans' father had a brother. And that brother had a son, who must have been your grandfather, Joseph Evans."

She looked over his shoulder as he traced through the Evans family history.

"Here's more, Heather. Your grandfather then had a daughter he named Bella, no doubt in honor of his drowned cousin. Then Bella married the baronet." He looked up at her, trying to make sense of it all. "But she must have died in Yorkshire, because her death is not recorded here. Let's see if we can find anything about you."

"Was I born here? Does it say?"

"No, you are not in here," he replied. "Since your father's estate was in Yorkshire, you were likely born there, just as your mother likely passed there. But it is also possible your mother brought you down here one summer before her death to visit her parents. We'll have to talk to their neighbors or village elders for confirmation. But

I'm sure she must have done so."

"I would like to see where my grandparents lived. I wonder if it will also appear familiar to me."

"It might. We will get there soon, I promise. Hopefully, the neighbors will have answers to our questions. We need to find out how old you were at the time, and what did you see that scared your family so badly, they resolved to keep you away from here forever?"

Heather's lips began to tremble, and Ruarke knew she would soon be in tears. "They took this drastic measure to protect you," he said. "How deeply they must have loved you. Why else would your grandparents never try to get in touch with you? Why else would your father never speak of them? He was not a cruel man. In fact, you described him as kind."

She nodded.

"He would not have cut off his own wife's family without good reason."

She drew out her locket and stared at it. "How did it come down to me?"

"We may never know, but it is possible my ancestor gave it to your mother because she shared Bella's name. A token, perhaps as he lay dying."

"Ruarke, I think I know how to break the haunting," Heather said. "There are two lockets. One your ancestor kept close to his heart and felt so strongly about that he included it in the painting hanging in your entry hall. That is the locket I now wear, and mistook the girl in it to be my mother. But Bella described another locket to me, the one he had given her that held his portrait."

"We don't have that one."

"Millicent stole it after she struck down Bella."

"Then it is likely lost to us forever. Who knows what she did with it?" Ruarke mused. "She could have tossed it into the sea, for all we know."

Heather began to nibble her lip. "What if we need both to free poor Bella? Do you think this is what keeps her bound to the caves? This is where the two of them secretly met. I'll wager James used to sneak out of the house through that secret tunnel you recently sealed up, so he would not be seen. But Bella now needs to reclaim the locket that contains his portrait. We must discover what happened to it."

"How? It is an impossible task. We wouldn't know where to start looking, assuming it hasn't been discarded or destroyed long since. But those lockets may not be the only way to free Bella. You are an Evans, Heather. I am a MacArran. I think it is significant that an Evans loves a MacArran."

"Just as those two loved each other in the past? Oh, of course! Do you think our marriage will be enough?"

Ruarke raked a hand through his hair. "It is possible."

Heather regarded him with loving eyes. "Is this not the most romantic thing ever to happen? We were fated to meet and fall in love, thereby closing the circle." She inhaled sharply and her eyes grew wide. "Does this mean you are in love with me?"

He smiled. "Seems so, doesn't it?"

Chapter Nine

AFTER SEVERAL HOURS of combing through the parish records, Ruarke knew there was no more information to be found in them. He rose and held out a hand to Heather. "We had better return to MacArran Grange or they'll be sending out a search party for us."

She nodded. "Your aunt will be screaming for me, no doubt."

"Let her scream. Your days in service to her are over. I'll move you into one of my guest quarters. In fact, I ought to put you beside me in the duchess suite of rooms."

"No." Her cheeks immediately turned a bright pink. "We are not yet married."

He sighed. "An oversight I hope to remedy, perhaps as early as tomorrow if you will allow it. I have no intention of waiting the month until the banns are read."

It was midday by the time they arrived back at the Grange. Ruarke's guests were milling about the dining room, eager for their next meal. "My apologies for keeping you waiting. Miss Alwyn and I—"

"The indecency!" His aunt barged forward like a bull. "Miss Alwyn, you are discharged. Pack up your things and leave at once."

"Miss Alwyn, don't you dare take a step," Ruarke shot back. "As for you, Aunt Lydia, since when is going to church to arrange for banns to be read indecent?"

"Church? Banns?"

"That's right. Be quiet, or you shall be the one sent packing. I had hoped to do this more gracefully, but it seems there is no point. Miss Alwyn and I are betrothed."

"What?" His cousin chuckled heartily and came forward to embrace him and then Heather. "Well done, Miss Alwyn. I was beginning to despair he would ever marry. Seems love is in the air, and now I might have to follow suit."

Ruarke grinned. "You are welcome to do so, Hereford. We just left the vicarage. In fact, my curricle remains at the ready should you have a mind to ride over. The vicar will be delighted to accommodate you."

His cousin turned to grin at a blushing Lady Sylvia. "That is good to know."

Several guests now came forward to congratulate Ruarke and Heather. Some appeared disappointed, but his aunt's look was venomous. "Why you scheming little—" She immediately broke off, no doubt realizing Heather would soon be his wife and hold sway over his purse strings. "Well, it is a shock," she stammered, now reconsidering and hastily attempting to make amends. "Of course, you shall be welcome into our family if this is my nephew's wish."

However, Miss Barclay was not so quick to embrace Heather's good fortune. She stepped forward with a smug expression on her face. "I would not be so quick to welcome her, Lady Audley. You worried she might be a thief, and now I must tell you that my necklace has been stolen."

Ruarke frowned. "Your necklace?"

"Yes, Your Grace. I saw that it was gone this morning and came looking for you to report it. I noticed Miss Alwyn by my door last night. I had just come up to retire to bed and thought it odd at the time. Now, I must insist her room be searched."

Heather's eyes widened. "But I didn't take it. I would never—"

Ruarke placed a comforting arm around her shoulders. "Hush, my girl. I know you are no thief." He summoned his housekeeper. "Mrs.

Pool, kindly go up to Miss Alwyn's room and search for an expensive-looking necklace. I am sure you will find it in an obvious spot. Miss Barclay, would you care to tell me exactly where Mrs. Pool might find it?"

"How would I know?" Miss Barclay asked.

"Because you planted it there. By the time you retired, Miss Alwyn was already in the kitchen attending to the trivial chores my aunt had requested be done last evening. She could not have been anywhere near your bedchamber."

The spiteful wasp would not back down. "That is an outrageous accusation! I know what I saw!"

"This should be interesting," Ruarke's cousin said, following him and Heather into his study along with Miss Barclay and her maiden aunt. Lady Audley followed as well, no doubt considering whose side to take. But since her comfortable style of living was dependent on his good graces, Ruarke expected her to sit quietly and only jump in once the outcome was obvious.

He turned to his other guests and held up a hand to keep them from following him in. "Please help yourself to the lavish repast awaiting you in the dining room. We shall not be long."

"I insist they stay on and witness Miss Alwyn's undoing," Miss Barclay said, her mouth curled in an ugly sneer.

"As you wish." Ruarke shrugged. "The truth will out."

Mrs. Pool returned with a locket in hand. "Is this the one? I am so sorry, Miss Alwyn. I know you did not take it. You were downstairs with me all that time. A dozen of His Grace's servants also saw you with me. You will be cleared of this."

"Thank you, Mrs. Pool." Heather emitted a soft cry the moment she saw the necklace in the housekeeper's outstretched hand, and then turned to Ruarke. "This is the twin of my locket."

"Hah! Now she is claiming to have one just like it." Miss Barclay huffed. "But it is mine."

"Indeed," her priggish aunt said. "It has been passed down the generations from mother to daughter since Millicent Barclay's day."

"Is that so?" Ruarke exchanged a look with Heather. He could not believe what the woman had just said. Did Heather understand the significance?

Now he glanced heavenward, for miracles did happen.

These Barclays were about to prove Millicent guilty of killing her own sister. The locket was identical to Heather's. Was it possible Millicent had kept it with her all these years? Just the sort of wickedness a mad sister might dream up. Not only to hold on to the necklace, but pass it to her heirs. How better to laugh at everyone, knowing she got away with murder?

But the locket would prove Millicent was at the caves with Bella that day and stole it off her neck after knocking the poor girl unconscious.

"Open it," he commanded Miss Pool, who still had it in her hand.

Miss Barclay glanced at it uncertainly. "There is nothing inside."

Ruarke frowned. "Are you certain?"

"Quite. It contains nothing inside." Her gaze was now brazen and combative as she tried to grab it away.

Ruarke took it instead and held it out of her reach. "Not a portrait of the Duke of Arran's son? The boy who loved Bella. He gave her a necklace identical to yours, which contained his portrait inside. If yours is empty, as you claim, then you will not mind if I open it and see what is inside."

"But I do mind." She tried to snatch it out of his hand again.

He easily held it out of her reach and now tried to open it, but his hands were big and awkward as he fumbled with the delicate clasp.

"Here, let me show you." Heather took it from him and easily opened it. "Dear heaven," she said in a breathless whisper, starting at the portrait it revealed.

He turned the full force of his fury on the Barclays. "Nothing inside? Then this one cannot possibly be yours, for it clearly has the portrait of a young man. My own granduncle, James. You dare to bring this locket into my home? This keepsake given to Millicent's sister by her true love. Bella always wore it. She was wearing it the day she died. That her sister had it and passed it on through your Barclay line only proves she was there with Bella that day at the caves."

"Your Grace, what are you suggesting?" Miss Barclay's outrage was now turning to fear as his words began to sink in.

"Was Millicent's secret carried down through the generations as well? Did you know she was a murderess? That she wore this locket after Bella's death for her own sick amusement because she hated her sister and had killed her? Get out of my house. Get out and never set foot in here again."

His words had shocked not only the Barclays, but all of his guests, who had ignored his earlier request to leave them to their private discussion. Apparently, a lavish meal set out for them in the dining room was no temptation when there was a scandal about to erupt. Miss Barclay had foolishly insisted they remain, thinking she was about to humiliate Heather. Instead, she had done herself in. The onlookers were now whispering excitedly among themselves.

"Bella got what she deserved," Miss Barclay said with a sneer, too full of venom to keep quiet and silently slip away. "She'll never be free of those caves."

With that, she and her aunt stormed off to pack their belongings.

"Good riddance," Ruarke muttered.

Heather's eyes shimmered with unshed tears. "They are wrong about Bella being trapped. This locket was never Millicent's to give away. I shall return it to its rightful owner." She withdrew her own locket, a perfect twin to the one in Ruarke's hand, and showed the others who were with them in the room. "This one belonged to my mother. I always thought it was a portrait of her, but it is Bella."

"Merciful heaven," Mrs. Pool muttered.

Heather nodded. "This is what Bella has been waiting for, the return of her locket. But I think I must give her mine as well. Two hearts reunited in love."

"I'll place them in the Singing Caves," Ruarke said. "But Heather, you must stay here. It is too dangerous for you to come with me."

Heather would not hear of it. "Bella won't hurt me now. I know she won't. You have to let me go to her. I must be there. Truly, how else is she to understand what we are doing?"

"No, Heather—"

"Who else can see her or speak to her? You cannot do this properly without me. Besides, I know I cannot come to harm when I have you to protect me."

Ruarke groaned. "You place too much faith in me."

She placed a hand lightly on his arm. "I know I shall always be safe with you."

"Low tide happens this evening, just before suppertime," Ruarke's cousin said.

Ruarke sighed. "Hereford, you always were a font of trivial information, but this time you've proved yourself quite useful."

೩

THE SUN SHONE late into the evening at this time of the year, so there was plenty of light as he and Heather made their way to the Singing Caves.

Heather held both lockets in her hand.

They were not the only ones present, for word had spread throughout the village. It seemed to Ruarke as though all its inhabitants were in attendance. The vicar was there with his wife and his prayer book. The curate was beside them with tears in his eyes.

Ruarke's houseguests also came along, for this would be quite a story to tell when they returned to London.

The vicar led the onlookers in prayer.

Ruarke was never one to pray, but perhaps tonight would change him.

The sky was an array of colors, of pinks and lavenders, as the sun began its descent on the horizon, and the sea sparkled. Ruarke climbed the rocks and held out his hand to help Heather onto them. "Are you sure about this? I can go in alone."

"I have to be with you. I am ready."

He could have ordered her to stay behind with the others, but she was right. He felt it as well. She *needed* to be with him.

He had brought a lantern along, and now lit it. "Here we go. Do not let go of my hand."

They entered the cave where Bella had drowned.

The ground was dank but mostly dry because the tide was out.

Heather took a deep breath. "Bella, we've brought you a gift. It is your missing locket. Your sweetheart had a similar one made for himself that held your portrait. They are both yours now. Take them with you as you cross over. It is time for you to go. James is waiting for you." She set them on a rocky ledge within the cave. "Be happy, Bella."

They waited a moment to see if their ghost would respond, but were met with silence.

Ruarke dared not remain inside any longer, even though there was still time before the tide came in. But he did not like the idea of Heather remaining in the cave another moment. "Let's go, love."

He led her back out.

They had just stepped down from the rocks and onto the sand when they heard a trill of laughter.

Heather gasped. "She's seen the necklaces."

"Good, now let's get you away from here," Ruarke muttered, and they quickly rejoined the onlookers at the other end of the beach.

He handed the lantern off to his cousin and wrapped his arms around Heather. Despite being certain they were doing the right thing, he would not manage a calming breath until Bella was gone.

Heather did not appear concerned and insisted they would soon see a sign. He had no idea what it might be. A dove flying overhead? A flash of light from inside the cave? A ghostly aura floating upward to heaven? Or nothing at all?

What if they were wrong and the return of the lockets did not work?

Heather grabbed hold of his hand and squeezed it. "It is happening."

He sucked in a breath. "What do you see?"

"They are both on the rocks, waving to us."

"Both?"

"Yes, Bella and James. He's come for her. Oh, Ruarke, he waited for her all these years." She waved back at them and blew Bella a kiss. "He looks so much like you. No wonder she fell in love with him."

"They are not us, Heather. I fell in love with *you*, not her," Ruarke said.

She looked at him with her eyes wide and glittering. "You called me *love* before in the cave. And now, are you... I thought... I..."

"You thought I only wanted you because you would make a good nanny?" He kissed the tip of her nose. "You probably would. But I am in love with you, Heather. You claimed my heart the moment I set eyes on you."

"Love at first sight?" She nodded. "This is how it was for me, too. Why did you not tell me sooner? Oh, I suppose you had to be cautious, considering you are the Duke of Arran and I could have been a scheming fortune hunter."

"I quickly saw that you were not."

"Look at that brilliant light," his cousin called out.

Ruarke turned his gaze heavenward.

Everyone was looking up now to *ooh* and *aah* as a fiery light shot across the darkening sky. "I think we must name it the MacArran-Evans comet," he said in jest.

Heather cast him an impish grin. "Or the Evans-MacArran comet."

He laughed. "So it shall be. I understand what they must be feeling. I would wait an eternity for you."

She looked up at him in wonder. "I would do the same for you." She nestled in his arms, her back against his chest as they watched the spectacle of light. "I love you, Ruarke."

He kissed her slender neck. "I love you, my elfin princess. By the way, I am marrying you tomorrow. Do not think to argue, for you shall never win this argument...although you will likely win every other one we shall ever have during our long and, dare I hope, mostly peaceful marriage."

True to his word, Ruarke obtained the license and they married in St. Augustine's Church the following morning, each of them vowing to love the other to the end of their days and beyond.

They held true to their vows.

THE END

Also by Meara Platt

FARTHINGALE SERIES
My Fair Lily
The Duke I'm Going To Marry
Rules For Reforming A Rake
A Midsummer's Kiss
The Viscount's Rose
Earl of Hearts
The Viscount and the Vicar's Daughter
A Duke For Adela
Marigold and the Marquess
The Make-Believe Marriage
If You Wished For Me
Never Dare A Duke
Capturing The Heart Of A Cameron

BOOK OF LOVE SERIES
The Look of Love
The Touch of Love
The Taste of Love
The Song of Love
The Scent of Love
The Kiss of Love
The Chance of Love
The Gift of Love
The Heart of Love
The Promise of Love
The Wonder of Love

The Journey of Love
The Treasure of Love
The Dance of Love
The Miracle of Love
The Hope of Love (novella)
The Dream of Love (novella)
The Remembrance of Love (novella)
All I Want For Christmas (novella)

MOONSTONE LANDING SERIES
Moonstone Landing (novella)
Moonstone Angel (novella)
The Moonstone Duke
The Moonstone Marquess
The Moonstone Major
The Moonstone Governess
The Moonstone Hero
The Moonstone Pirate

DARK GARDENS SERIES
Garden of Shadows
Garden of Light
Garden of Dragons
Garden of Destiny
Garden of Angels

SILVER DUKES
Cherish and the Duke
Moonlight and the Duke
Two Nights with the Duke

LYON'S DEN
The Lyon's Surprise
Kiss of the Lyon

Lyon in the Rough

THE BRAYDENS
A Match Made In Duty
Earl of Westcliff
Fortune's Dragon
Earl of Kinross
Earl of Alnwick
Tempting Taffy
Aislin
Genalynn
Pearls of Fire*
A Rescued Heart
*also in Pirates of Britannia series

DeWOLFE PACK ANGELS SERIES
Nobody's Angel
Kiss An Angel
Bhrodi's Angel

About the Author

Meara Platt is a USA Today bestselling author and an award winning, Amazon UK All-star. Her favorite place in all the world is England's Lake District, which may not come as a surprise since many of her stories are set in that idyllic landscape, including her award winning, fantasy romance Dark Gardens series. If you'd like to learn more about the ancient Fae prophecy that is about to unfold in the Dark Gardens series, as well as Meara's lighthearted, international bestselling Regency romances in the Farthingale series and Book of Love series, or her more emotional Moonstone Landing series and Braydens series, please visit Meara's website at www.mearaplatt.com.

Made in the USA
Columbia, SC
05 June 2025

59007132R00050